RESCUER

Stefanie Dawn

Rescuer
Elements of Abduction
Book 2

Stefanie Dawn

This book is a work of fiction. Any references to real events, real people, and real places are used fictitiously. Other names, characters, places and incidents are products of the Author's imagination and any resemblance to persons, living or dead, actual events, organizations or places is entirely coincidental.

All rights are reserved. This book is intended for the purchaser of this book ONLY. No part of this book may be reproduced or transmitted in any form or by any means, graphic, electronic, or mechanical, including photocopying, recording, taping, or by any information storage retrieval system, without the express written permission of the Author. All songs, song titles and lyrics contained in this book are the property of the respective songwriters and copyright holders.

Disclaimer: The material in this book contains graphic language and sexual content and is intended for mature audiences, ages 18 and older.

ISBN: 978-1763870499

Editing and Proofing by Swish Design & Editing
Book Design by Swish Design & Editing
Cover Design by Eric at
The Book Brander
Published by Angels and Fire Books
Cover Image Copyright 2023

First Edition
Copyright © 2023 Angels and Fire Books
All Rights Reserved

DEDICATION

To all those who proudly read monster-fucker
books and don't give a rat's what anyone thinks.
We've found our people—we know the deal.

RESCUER

CHAPTER

I

TORI

Bullshit.

Absolute bullshit.

Bullshit was my mother's favorite curse word, and she said it often—several times a day when we were back on the farm, rarely in its literal context. It usually began with several utterings an hour during milking in the morning because Mom's cows were as stubborn as her.

Feeling the farm life hadn't been for me, I moved to the city as soon as I could afford it. But that old saying about being able to take the *girl from the country but not the country from the girl* was apparently true. I hadn't made many close friends either because I constantly felt out of place.

Or maybe it's because I'd generally made myself unlikeable to people.

"This is bullshit!"

My mother's favorite word was now mine too and was screamed from my lungs with as much force as I could muster, among other choice words, as I was dragged from my home.

I'd gotten out of bed to use the bathroom and didn't even get a chance to wash my hands before I was knocked to the floor from the force of a blast which, while it was strong enough to throw me from my feet, was silent apart from the clatter of the roof tiles hitting the floor before they shattered. I should have run, but curiosity got the better of me, and I stepped out of the small bathroom and under the brand-new circular hole in my apartment ceiling and looked up.

And found myself staring into a white light.

A handful of things came to my mind about what it could be in that instant, and none of them were *good* options. I ran, but it was too little too late and got caught in an invisible beam. I was being dragged from my home, clinging to any surface I could latch onto along the way. None of it made a difference, and the sound of every item on my dressing table hitting the floor added to my screams as I desperately tried to cling to the anchor. I gripped so hard onto the edge of the hole in the ceiling as I swooped through it I thought I was going to break my fingernails clean off before I was eventually forced to let go.

Once in the open, I didn't fight the upside-down freefall and simply yelled, "Well, this is fucking *bullshit,*" as I tumbled through the night air and was taken aboard a fucking alien spacecraft. The shutter closed beneath my feet before I was dumped unceremoniously onto the ice-cold floor. My robe was thick, but it was not enough to stop my teeth from chattering even as I pulled it tighter around me. The cold was so intense my bare feet felt like they were burning on the floor, and I hopped from foot to foot, muttering obscenities and looking around for a way out or someone I could yell at to answer some of my more pressing questions.

Like, *what the fuck was this fucking bullshit?*

Did aliens understand swearing?

If not, I'm sure they'd understand a swift punch to their alien faces.

There was silence, the kind of silence that echoes around an empty space and feels like it's pressing against your eardrums. The sound of my light steps as I bounced from foot to foot, scanning the ceiling and the walls for any means of escape or a weapon, bounced off the smooth walls and came back to me magnified. After a quiet whoosh, I froze, and my spine stiffened before I found the strength to turn around. A door had slid open, appearing in an otherwise unmarked wall, and a group of people stood at the door.

No, not people.

Biting into the fleshy part of my hand, I tried to curtail my terror. Terror that rushed into every pore along with the stinging cold of the spaceship. Terror I had been able to deny with indignant rage until the moment I laid eyes on the beings who had taken me.

Because they made it real.

These couldn't be people. They weren't like any people I'd ever seen. They were small with wide bodies, pear-shaped and ending on short, stumpy legs and large, flat feet. They were wearing space suits, but when one of them looked directly at me, I saw an eye through the window on its helmet. Just one eye, almost as large as its entire head, a sickly yellowish-green color, like it was sticky and infected. My stomach churned, and I wanted to retch, but what I didn't want to do was turn my back on the aliens as they approached me. I backed against the far wall, but they kept coming, seemingly unconcerned with my fear. Small hands that felt like rubber suckers grabbed my arms and pulled. I leaned away from their grip, hoping my weight alone would be enough to stop them from moving me because God knows I couldn't get much grip on this floor with no shoes.

My efforts meant nothing, and the aliens pulled

until I was almost yanked off my feet before I relented and stilled, gritting my teeth and walking alongside them as we exited the room. The second we crossed the threshold, I began fighting anew, more space meaning more area to swing, but they simply had more of them hold my arms still, and kicking did nothing but lift me off the floor momentarily.

"Get off me, you swine." I fought them the entire way and was still fighting them when the door from the room we had left slid shut behind me with the same quiet whoosh. As we moved down a short hallway, sterile and plain, a white so bright it looked like the light was coming from the walls themselves, I continued to fight. My arms were beginning to hurt from the constant yanking against their sticky grip by the time we entered a larger room, but I didn't stop pulling against them, and when I took the briefest moment to look around, my jaw dropped.

A flat slab of whatever metal the ship was made of floated in the middle of the room, and I was pushed toward it. When they tried to make me lie down on the table, I screamed again, letting go a string of obscenities, some of which I'm not even sure were real words as I fought. When they got a single strap around my wrist, I knew it was over, and as they pulled and tightened the restraint, I was forced to move closer to the table, now swiping out with only one free arm. It was only a matter of time before other straps were attached to my ankles, thighs, and upper arms. Bit by bit, I was forced to lie and was held still against the cold table, shivering and crying. There was no stopping the tears at this point, and honestly, I'm surprised I managed to hold them back this long. If not for the throbbing pain in my arm and the stinging of my bare feet, I could have perhaps told myself this was a nightmare, and if I closed my eyes tight enough, I would wake up at home.

But no.

As I turned my head to the side, another tremble shuddered through my body as my cheek pressed against the cold metal, torn between wanting to see what was in store for me and looking away and pretending it wasn't happening. One of the aliens approached with a white instrument, maybe seven inches long. "Please," I whispered. Since screaming and yelling did nothing, maybe they would stop if I tried talking to them. "Please don't hurt me. Just leave me alone. I want to go home."

It was ironic now that the only place I wanted to be was home since I'd done nothing but complain about it to myself, as I had no one else to complain to or who really paid attention. As a hairdresser, I was chatty, but people only wanted to talk about themselves. They didn't come to the salon to hear my problems about how hopelessly single I was or my trust issues. They didn't want to hear about my mother losing her mind to dementia and my subsequent guilt for leaving her to run the farm on her own so long before she was diagnosed. I'd convinced myself she somehow would've been okay if only I'd stayed longer. The doctors could tell me otherwise all they wanted, but in my mind, I didn't do enough. I'd abandoned her in pursuit of my selfish desires to find something *more,* realizing too late that true happiness was in simplicity. Now, she was in a nursing home in the country because she hated the city, and I couldn't get out to see her very often. The nurses assured me she was happy, even if she didn't know who they were.

Or who I was when I visited.

I was lonely, and I didn't realize how lonely until I could no longer talk to my mom.

The tears came faster when I realized she wouldn't miss me because she didn't remember me.

That was okay. I didn't want her to be sad if I died.

I didn't want her to think I'd abandoned her *again.*

All this stuff always swirled around in my head, and I had no one to talk to it about. Clients wanted to talk about their children, their husbands, and the most recent gossip at their workplace or with their neighbors, and not about my bullshit.

The aliens ignored my pleas and tears, and I

squeezed my eyes shut, thinking of a simpler and better time. How when I was eleven, I used paint made with food-safe dye to paint the cows with colorful patterns, and Mom laughed and joked the milk would be a rainbow swirl.

But I couldn't rid my mind of the worst-case scenario images of how today might end. The probe they held was first shoved into my ear, pressing hard enough until a cry broke past my gritted teeth. Then they repeated it on the other ear. The aliens made no sound during this process, not talking to themselves or me.

The probe was then placed near my lips, and I pressed them together in a tight line. The alien holding the probe made an impatient noise and pressed until I could feel my teeth pushing painfully against the inside of my lips. But I still didn't open my mouth. With another noise, the alien slapped my cheek, a small series of light slaps with his sticky glove. Despite the sting, I still refused to open my mouth, my eyes watering. The alien leaned over me, its giant green eyeball staring at my face. The sight made me shudder, but also angry.

Fuck you, alien.

Which I couldn't say because that would be giving them exactly what they wanted by opening my mouth.

The alien's other hand slowly came up and stopped over my face. I was tempted to try to bite its fingers, but that also would mean opening my mouth. My chest was heaving, bursts of hot hair coming from my nostrils as I held my mouth closed against the probe as it pressed against my lips. The alien's fingers went to my nose, and my eyes widened as it clamped my nostrils closed.

I squeezed my eyes shut.

I couldn't breathe.

But I wouldn't give in.

Pulling against the restraints, I bucked my hips and legs trying to loosen them. My lungs started to burn, and my head spun as I became desperate for oxygen. The sickly green eyeball was still staring at me when I opened my eyes, and I closed them again.

I thought my chest was going to explode. My brain was screaming at me for air, damn the consequences.

The second I opened my mouth to gasp for air, the probe was shoved in, knocking against and possibly chipping one of my teeth with the force. My nose was released, and I sucked in grateful lungfuls of air while glaring at the alien. The probe was maneuvered around my mouth, hitting the sides of my inner cheeks and pressed under my tongue. When it was pulled from my mouth, the alien tilted its head to the side as if to say *see, that wasn't so bad.*

"Fuck you," I spat out. But once again, it ignored me and flipped open my robe before yanking up my night shirt. I bucked against the restraints again.

"Get your fucking hands off me!"

The probe was pressed against my belly button, rotating around and pressing hard until I was certain it was going to puncture clean through my stomach. It wasn't over when it lifted the probe, either. Instead, it was followed by bringing it down harder several times, stabbing against my belly button, causing me to cry out in pain and the tears to start again.

Then it was over, and they were moving away from the table.

The straps slid off my arms and legs on their own, and I sat, cradling my tender stomach in my palms and taking a moment to steady my shaky breathing and run my tongue along my teeth, checking for a chip.

The aliens approached me again.

"What the fuck do you want now?" It felt good to swear so openly. I often curbed the sailor talk while at work, but this was no time to hold back. I was fucking *pissed*, and I wanted these little assholes to know it. I slapped a gloved hand away when one of them reached for me, and it hesitated for only a moment before its hand shot toward me again, gripping my wrist and forcing me to slide myself from the table.

As I was led from the room and back into the short hallway, I was steered toward the door at the opposite end, and all I could think of was *when is this going to fucking end?* The adrenaline was wearing off, and my emotions were all over the place, swinging wildly between anger and fear and acceptance that I might die here.

Or worse.

Another quiet whoosh, another set of doors opened, and I lifted my head slowly to take in the room. The second my eyes had adjusted to the light, I started fighting again.

There were several large, clear cubes, each floating slightly off the ground, and in one of them was another woman, her hands pressed against the clear sides, watching me intently. There was fear in her eyes, which I'm sure was reflected in my expression. Her long brown hair fell over her shoulders and face, and summery night clothes were all she wore. When our eyes met, she started slapping her hands against the side of the cube, and I could tell she was screaming only by looking at her face, but there was no sound.

"Oh fuck no!" I wiggled harder then, and when the aliens' sticky grip on my arms loosened, I yanked hard. With one arm free from their hold, I was able to swipe at the others, and they jumped out of the way, letting me go to avoid being slapped or kicked.

I bolted, not even sure where I was running to, but I knew I wasn't going into some cage without a fight. There were several aliens around a large, flat black screen, which was blank except for the occasional unfamiliar figure that popped up. There were no dials or buttons, so I simply ran to the screen and started slapping my hands against it, wanting *anything* to happen that would lend itself to my escape. There was an explosion of sound behind me, angry clicking and squawking as the aliens came at me again. Was I annoying them by touching their precious panel? *Good.* Maybe I would, at the very least, cause some damage. I fought them off with one hand while I continued to touch everything I could reach on the desk, hoping to send the ship into a soaring spiral.

If I'm going down, I'm taking you all with me.

Their numbers soon overwhelmed me, and I was dragged toward one of the cubes.

But I didn't stop fighting, and eventually, one came at me with a weapon of some sort, and after a sharp and searing pain on my head, everything went black.

CHAPTER 2

TORI

My head was throbbing, and who was the idiot who left the light on? Or had I slept through the night and well into the following day? It wouldn't surprise me, not with the messed-up dreams I had.

My stomach hurt too, and I pressed my hand tenderly against my belly, jolting it away when the pain increased like I was bruised.

Why would my stomach be bruised?

Bull... shit...

Even though my head throbbed as I stood rapidly, I didn't stop and paced my cube—my prison— slowly picking up speed until I was running around the edges in tight circles, slamming my fists against the clear walls and screaming at the aliens who milled around the outside. But much like the other woman's screams, they couldn't hear me, and if they could, I doubt they would have cared anyway. I placed my hands around my throat. The air was thin in here, and I was certain I was choking. My breathing was coming in small, shallow gasps, and if I didn't get it under control soon, I was going to pass out again. In my peripheral vision, I saw the woman in the cube nearest to mine sink to her knees as I did, her hands pressed against the cube as if she wanted to reach out and help me, but she couldn't help. She couldn't save me any more than I could save her or myself or stop the aliens from probing and sticking me in this fucking cage.

Gasping for air, I curled up into a ball, and when the gasps turned into sobs, I let the tears come because, at that moment, I couldn't think of a single thing I could do other than cry.

Okay, enough with this crying bullshit.

Sitting up, I rubbed my face vigorously with my palms and looked over to find the other woman staring at me. She had her legs tucked neatly under her, and when she caught my eye, she lifted her hand in possibly the saddest wave I'd ever seen in my life. She pointed at her stomach and lifted her flimsy T-shirt to reveal bruising around her belly button. I copied, showing her my stomach. I guess we were both assaulted with that damn probe in the same way. After she dropped her T-shirt, she frowned, and I wished we were in the same damn cube so we could talk.

We simply leaned against the corners of our cubes as close as we could get to each other. I don't think I've ever sought the closeness of a stranger before, but now I'd give anything to hug this woman. She looked lost and afraid, and I wondered if my expression was the same, and I just didn't know it yet.

I wondered what her name was.

With my head against the side of the cube, which was mercifully warmer than the ship outside, I watched my breath fog up.

"That's it!" I slapped my palm against the side of the cube, and although I knew she couldn't hear me, I kept doing it for a few seconds until the other woman looked up. I held my finger up at her and then pointed to my mouth. Breathing on the side of the cube, it fogged up, and I quickly spelled out *name?*

The word faded, and her eyes widened. She

repeated my actions.

Erica.

My turn. *Tori.* Glad I went by Tori for so long now. Victoria would've taken too long to write out, and I barely had the energy to maintain my excitement at being able to communicate with Erica.

Her smile was small, barely a lift of her lips, and her eyes sad.

Hi.

Hi.

That was all we said for several hours.

The time passed slowly, and two other girls were brought in to join Erica and me. Shortly after, there was a heavy whirring underneath us. It somehow felt like vibrations through our feet despite the floating cubes, which I took to mean the ship was moving.

Great.

Misha, who had come in after me, had dark hair that sat in tight curls around her face, and her expression was determined and fearful at the same time. She looked like a country girl. Don't ask me how I knew—I just had a feeling. There was something about the way she walked, even when she was being half-dragged by some asshole aliens. Or I could've been drawing conclusions from the cowboy hat and horseshoe print on her night clothes. Maybe the girl just liked horses, I didn't know. Last to come in was Samara, who I found out later was only nineteen and mostly hid her face behind her blonde hair. But even that couldn't hide the fear clear in her expression.

My anger only increased after each girl was brought in. Who the fuck did these aliens think they were?

The aliens came in twice a day and gave us food but no water. It was only after giving in and trying the jelly-like white substance that we discovered it served as both, quenching our thirst and hunger at the same time. At one point, we tried to escape by grabbing onto the aliens when they went to feed us, but this only resulted in Erica being poisoned. I thanked God she didn't die, then wondered if it may have been better if she did.

Nothing changed for about a week. We were fed, and the little containers in the corner of our respective cubes that served as toilets emptied even though no one ever came in to do so. Then one day, they didn't come with our morning food. I exchanged a glance with Erica because this couldn't be a good thing. While our situation was dire, routine was at least some level of comfort, and the second that changed, it meant something was up.

Then the aliens came for us.

The doors of the cubes had been opened, and the room was suddenly filled with the sounds of four women screaming as the aliens filed into our cages, working simultaneously and overwhelming us in numbers in order to restrain us. So I did what I had been doing every single time those little assholes placed their hands on me—I fought. I had a week's worth of pent-up anger and fear, and I fought *hard,* kicking out and punching at every one of the little suckers I could reach. I exited the cube willingly because it was the closest thing to freedom I had felt, but I wouldn't go another step with them. I wanted to go in the opposite direction to where they were leading us. I had no idea what was that way, but it didn't matter. All that mattered was it was *not* where they wanted us to go, and dammit, if it wasn't the only form of rebellion I had.

I fought. Until one of them jammed something into my back, and a shock almost equivalent to a cattle prod shot through me, stiffening my spine and causing me to cry out. As they came and grabbed my arms, I weakly tried to swat them away, but I was weary of the weapon they now kept waving in front of my face. Evidently, they were sick of my shit and wanted things to go smoother this time.

The girls and I were separated and brought to

different rooms, and still having jolts from the pain of the shock up my spine, I allowed myself to be led into the room and placed on the same table I had before. The restraints came up and clamped me down, and I lay there in silence as the pain subsided.

With a buzzing sound, the table I was lying on began shifting, and while I tried not to imagine what fresh horrors could be waiting for me now, even the burning from the cold metal against my skin wasn't enough to distract me from reality.

The table continued to shift, and my legs were forced to bend at the knees. With the smooth buzz continuing, my legs were spread open. "Oh fuck, no!" I cried out, yanking my knees against the restraints, and even though my mind was telling me it was no good, that they were too strong, I couldn't bring myself to stop trying. "No, no, no, *no, no, no!*"

Bucking against the restraints was painful, but any pain brought on by trying to escape would surely be better than whatever it was they had planned. And I had a pretty good idea what it was they were thinking. The aliens approached me with a different tool this time, and I realized I was a fool to allow myself to be strapped down without a fight.

Because this was not the same probe.

The instrument was spiraled and thick, almost

two feet long with a round nodule at the tip. I didn't stop struggling, but the binds were so tight my legs and hips barely moved at all, staying firmly in place against the table as the aliens cut away the crotch of my pajama pants.

I stared at the round nodule of the instrument, and bile rose in my throat. The inside of it swirled with a thick white substance, and I couldn't keep looking at it, but I couldn't look away.

Tadpoles.

Fucking alien sperm tadpoles.

"Fuck this shit!" I screamed and struggled. The binds were cutting into my wrists, but I didn't care. They could cattle prod me all they wanted, but there was nothing that would stop me from fighting. I thought about the other women, and my heart pined for them.

The instrument whirred to life, and I watched, refusing to accept my helplessness as two of the aliens peered between my legs.

Then, they stopped.

I held my breath and ceased my struggles, not daring to move in the silence that abruptly encompassed the room.

There were a few faint clicks and screeches between them, but mostly silence. The two closest to me moved away, and another three came closer, placing their horrible hands on my thighs and peering between my legs, their green eyes nearer to my pussy than I would like. But I still didn't move. One of them reached out a finger and pressed it against my labia, and I cried out, "Hey! What the shit do you think you're doing?"

The green eye came to land upon me, and I stared it down.

More silence.

Then several things happened in quick succession.

The restraints were gone, and I was dragged from the table, out of the room, and into the hallway. The aggravated chatter of the aliens got louder as we were joined by the other groups of aliens and the girls, who looked equally as alarmed and confused as I felt. When we were shoved into a small, round room, I turned to face our kidnappers, ready to fight, but they kept pushing and shoving us until we were almost backed against the wall. At one point, Erica reached out a hand toward me before her arm was slapped down by one of the aliens. We exchanged a pained look as pods emerged from the walls, and we were shuffled toward them.

They were dumping us.

The screaming recommenced as we were shoved into the pods, and once the door slid shut, I couldn't hear anything going on outside. With a sickening lurch that brought my stomach up to my throat, I barely had time to register what was happening before the pod shot backward and tumbled through space.

They were abandoning us in space. Why?

The vision outside my small window spun, revealing stars and galaxies before, upside down, I was presented with a planet in front of me—familiar greens and blues and the white swirls of cloud cover over the round planet. "Holy shit, is that Earth?" My voice broke as I cried out.

It looked too good to be true. Was our ordeal over?

No.

I may not have been a scholar, but I wasn't an idiot nor was I much of an optimist. A bright orange sun and no sign of cities or civilization on the unfamiliar continent meant we were still very fucking far away from home.

And about to crash-land on an alien planet.

I watched the other pods disappear and gripped the small chair I was awkwardly sitting on until my knuckles went white. My plummet to the planet's surface was interrupted by another jolt, and then I drifted toward the surface.

So the aliens wouldn't let us splat against the surface of a strange planet, having fitted the pods with what I can only assume was some sort of parachute to make sure we landed softly.

No splatting against the ground. Good.

Only the small problem of being abandoned and

to fend for ourselves.

"This is why I'm not an optimist," I muttered into the silence.

CHAPTER 3

TORI

At least I landed, and I was alive. That's the extent of me looking on the bright side, and given the current situation, I'm surprised I mustered even the energy for that.

The downside was I was alone on an alien planet, and that was a pretty fucking big downside. After having been kidnapped by some asshole aliens, I was on a random planet, and to top it off, I was stuck in a tree. Was this my abductors' home planet? Would there be a welcome party to come meet me and finish the procedure that the aliens on the ship had almost started? No, thank you. I was *not* staying here and waiting for them to find me. Or for anyone to find me, for that matter. If I were going to be found, it would be on my terms, and I would want to watch anyone for a while before I approached them.

Assuming I found anyone at all.

The door of the pod slid open. I scrambled against the seat, wedging myself behind it as when the pod had crashed into a tree, it had tilted, and the door was facing straight down toward the ground. I hadn't done anything to open the door, and so I waited there, crouched behind the seat for a while, listening for the telltale sign of anything approaching. There was a lot of background chatter, what could be whatever this planet's equivalent of birds and small animals foraging. But I heard nothing that sounded like speech nor anything large coming my way. I couldn't hear vehicles or aliens with sickly green eyes and large, flat feet wearing white space suits.

I studied the branches before me to see if I could map a way down.

Do you remember climbing trees as a child? And when you see a tree as an adult, you reminisce about how fun it was to climb it? Then you realize that climbing trees is hard work without your childhood nimbleness, the fact you were lighter and smaller, and an unwavering faith that no matter what, Mom will come and save you.

Still, I'm stubborn.

The tree was all green, the deep, uneven color across every trunk and twig, and the branches curled and twisted over each other. There were no leaves I could see, at least from where I was, but the entire thing seemed to be covered in some sort of mossy texture. Hopefully, it was soft—that would make this a bit easier. Twisting around, I lowered myself from the pod until my toes brushed the branch below me. It didn't feel like moss like I was expecting, but it wasn't unpleasant either, feeling almost like wool on a sheep, slightly oily and wiry but not harsh.

My personal trainer had been pushing me hard to increase my upper body strength lately, and although I muttered things under my breath, called him every name under the sun, and *hated* him while I was working out, I was thankful for it now. Able to lower myself gently, I placed both feet on the branch below, curling my toes against the curvature of the wood and hoping it would hold me. Slowly, I let go of the pod, hovering my arms out near it, ready to grab on if there was even a hint that the branch was going to break under my weight. But it didn't, and I breathed a sigh of relief.

First step done.

Next step, get to the ground without breaking my neck.

Sighing again, I looked down at my clothes. I didn't want to ditch my robe because who knows how cold this planet would get, but climbing down a tree with it on was asking for trouble. So, balancing myself, I took off my robe and balled it up, tossing it to the ground and watching its trajectory. Hopefully, it was still there when I got down.

I turned around and lowered myself until I was crouching and my hands were on the same branch I stood on. Then, just as slowly as I had lowered myself from the pod, I repeated the motion until my feet touched the next branch down.

And repeat and repeat.

Eleven times until I finally reached the ground.

Looking around, I frowned. There was no white cotton amongst the green of the forest floor. My gown was gone. *Fuck.* I rolled my shoulders, trying not to be unsettled by the idea that something had swooped in and grabbed my robe without me hearing them, but also that they had been close enough to get in and out while I was descending the tree.

It felt like I was being watched, and I rubbed my palms up and down my forearms—the shiver running down my spine having nothing to do with the temperature.

Nope, this was no time to descend into hopelessness.

Next step—find shelter.

Or food, or water, or whatever came first.

While not the most positive person, I decided to mentally write a list of pros and cons of my immediate situation. Pro of being in a forest, lots of material to build a shelter and weapons with. Con, possibly lots of creatures I would need to defend myself against. Con, I had lost my robe. Pro, the weather wasn't unpleasant. Con, I didn't know what the weather would do when it got dark. Con, I didn't know a lot of things. Con, I was hopelessly lost. Con, there may be no friendly life on this planet. Con, there may be no life at all. Con, even if there was, I may never find them. Con, I may starve to death.

Okay, so much for the pros and cons list.

Stretching out my aching muscles, I shook my legs out and took a few tentative steps away from the tree. The ground was spongy beneath my feet, but again, not unpleasant. Humming quietly to myself to stop from going insane, I began my search for one of the three things I needed to survive this place. The roots of the trees were huge and dived in and out of the soil, some high enough I needed to duck through the space underneath, others I could step or clamber over. It was impossible to tell which root system belonged to which tree.

Leaves rustled behind me, and my humming ceased abruptly as I turned but saw no movement. Turning back, the rustling started again, and I kept humming. But my gait was stiff now, and my eyes scanned the ground for anything I could use as a weapon. I played cat and mouse with whatever the hell was following me for a while, the sound ceasing every time I stopped and turned but definitely getting closer when I continued to walk. I moved faster but didn't run, not wanting to entice a chase with some random creature. It sounded small, moving underneath all the roots I needed to step over. Finally, I spotted a fallen branch, small enough for me to wield but large enough to do damage, and I picked it up, closing my fingers around the rough green surface and holding it ready like a baseball bat.

The scuttling increased, now accompanied by a grunting noise I did *not* like the sound of.

There was a squeal, and I spun, swinging my makeshift bat out in front of me. The branch collided with the small creature midair, which went flying and hit the nearest tree trunk with a sickening crunch before it landed on the ground. Cautiously, I moved over to it. It looked almost like a beaver, but instead of two large front teeth, its mouth hung open to reveal three rows of razor-sharp blade-like teeth. Its neck was at an odd angle, and its two legs—its only limbs—were still.

I had killed it.

It was difficult to feel bad, especially looking now at the rows of teeth that would've made quick work of my skin.

My stomach rumbled, and wearily, I glanced at the alien beaver. Shrugging, I picked up the corpse by one of its legs, and when it didn't move, I slung it over my shoulder.

Food is food, I guess.

Time to make a fire.

CHAPTER
4

VITRI

Standing in the shadows, I clung to the soft fabric I had picked up as I watched the female collect her kill and continue to move through the forest. She had impressed me. When I had run toward the landing site after seeing the unit drop from the sky and witnessed her descent from the tree, she had appeared so small and fragile. I expected her to scream and hide at the first sight of anything alien to her, but she hadn't. Her instinct had been to get a weapon and kill whatever attacked her.

I didn't know the name of her species or what

planet she came from, but I knew she was the one. My brother had told me the Ghaal—the native species on this planet, violent and on the edge of extinction—had found the species compatible with them for breeding. We knew one day, somehow, they would find a way to bring some females here to use.

It seems the Ghaal had succeeded.

My first instinct was to leap out, snatch up the female, and run her back to my home to protect her. But it appeared her looks were deceiving. Maybe it was a trap, and she used her fragile and soft looks to draw victims in before attacking them. Maybe she held some sort of physical defense system I couldn't see.

I was intrigued but cautious. I knew nothing of her except the danger she was in from the Ghaal. I would protect her but from a distance.

For now.

Lifting the white fabric to my face, I inhaled her scent—soft, delicate, and feminine. It stirred a part of me I had kept dormant for many years. My instinct was to claim and breed, and this female made my cock harden even watching her.

But I wasn't an animal.

I wasn't in the lab anymore. I was my own being, and I wouldn't break again.

I would control myself.

As she moved through the forest, picking up

twigs along her way, I followed, keeping to the shadows. It wasn't difficult for me to blend in. As a Synth, I adapted physically to my environment, kind of like an advanced evolution, and years in this forest had made me one with it. My skin was the same deep green as the trees but hard enough to withstand the worst weather and attacks this place could throw at me. There were vines now—I don't even remember when they formed—but they were part of me, growing from my spine and winding themselves around my torso and arms when not in use. I had learned to control them over time—they were a part of me and simply other limbs.

The female stopped when she came to a clearing, casting a look around her, her gaze passing right over where I stood without pausing before she sank to her knees and cleared a space.

She was making a fire, and I was impressed again.

There were many species dropped on our planet that were not native here, kidnapped from their homes by the Moeks, and, if not useful to them, dropped here for the Ghaals to test. My brothers and I tried to look after those we could, communicate the dangers of the planet and the Ghaal colony to them and, if we could, teach them how to survive. But there had been few we could communicate well enough with, and most we simply resorted to scaring away from the Ghaal colony between the mountains and the sea because any new species would be safest if they never encountered a Ghaal.

Although they had been waiting for the return of *this* female species, they would experiment on any the Moeks dropped. The Ghaal became more desperate for a solution to their declining numbers with every day that passed.

I was intrigued by this female. She didn't look unlike me, in a basic sense—two arms, two legs, two eyes, and a scent that stirred my instinct. She smelled purely feminine, and I felt my cock swell further at the sight of her building the fire. I could tell she was strong for her species, and things I hadn't thought about in a long time came to the surface. I was a being *designed* for breeding, and *this* female brought out that part of me, stronger and more insistent than I had experienced in years.

But I would have to ignore it and drive it back down because my duty was only to ensure she was cared for and safe and nothing more.

Eventually, she got a fire going and speared the barda—a young one, less than a third of the size it would get to—through with a long stick and held it over the fire. I frowned. She didn't skin it, but I supposed she had no way to. I glanced down at my hands like every other part of me was larger than her, and if I stood next to her, the top of her head would barely reach my chest. Perhaps her fingers and claws weren't strong enough to skin the creature. My fingers twitched against the tree as I planted my hands on either side of me to lean forward and watch her closer. I could help her, but my appearance might frighten her. Perhaps she would attack me.

The idea of that stirred something in me that definitely wasn't fear and not an ideal reaction to be having toward a female I should be thinking nothing too deeply of.

Maybe she would try to fight me off—maybe it would be a game to her.

Maybe she would play with me.

Maybe she would allow me to play with her.

It was best to watch for now to see if she could fend for herself and if I needed to interfere at all.

As the barda cooked, she was mumbling to herself. A language with unfamiliar syllables, I ran a few of the words silently around in my mouth. They were strange, but I could learn them if she would let me. It would take only a few minutes—I could connect with her mind and learn to communicate with her. The indecision held me back. She had been on the planet only a short time and would still be frightened.

I found I couldn't leave her alone and had to keep watching. As long as I was close, I knew she would be safe because I could fend off any further threats to her and stop her if she went to eat or drink something dangerous. My gaze was glued to her movements, her delicate limbs, how soft her skin looked, and her dark hair that trailed down her back.

Running my hands through my braids, I almost smiled. I could braid her hair like mine, and then maybe she would lay with me and let me join with her mind.

She needed time, and I was content to watch her for now.

CHAPTER 5

TORI

It knocks it out of you, this whole being-abducted-by-aliens thing. Eating the alien beaver had been more of an effort than I had anticipated. I had no means of skinning it and hoped the fire would burn away more of the fur, but it was tough and wiry with long roots that dug into the creature's skin farther than any follicles I had ever seen. By that point, it had become a personal challenge, and I wouldn't give up until I had eaten my fill. I was starting to feel a twinge of guilt for killing the creature, and it would seem worse if I didn't make use of the meat.

Pulling the fur from the thing as it cooked was tedious since I had no knives and couldn't see any stones I could sharpen. I simply had to wait until the fur charred, which smelled about as good as you would expect, and yank it off in burned tufts, using what was left of my fingernails to dig the deep cuticles from the meat like tiny bones. Admittedly, once the fur was off and the meat was cooked, the taste wasn't so bad, even if the texture was like eating an old boot.

Once I had eaten my fill and left the remainder of the carcass on the fire to burn down, exhaustion took over. It was difficult to relax since every background sound was a reminder I wasn't home, and there were likely many dangers here I hadn't seen the likes of. But as I sat by the fire, the warmth from the embers washing over me, my eyelids began to droop. Glancing up, the strangely orange sun was nearing the horizon. I must have been walking for longer than I thought and wished I had landed near the other girls or at least been able to see where their pods went. But once through the line of the clouds, I had lost sight of them as my pod spun away.

While it would seem foolish to wander a strange planet in search of them, I didn't see what difference it made anyway. Staying here and surviving would be purely existing, and that wasn't any kind of life I wanted to maintain in the long term. Even if I wandered until I starved, at least I tried to find them and regain some sense of normality. If I were to find them, we could work together, build a shelter together, and maybe see if there were any aliens on this planet who could help us get back to Earth.

Being alone never bothered me back home, but now, it was a burden that weighed heavily in my chest.

Realizing I couldn't stay awake much longer, I stood and looked around for somewhere to sleep. Kicking some soil over the remnants of the fire, I moved back to the nearest tree with those large roots and searched around the base until I found a nook barely big enough to get into. I figured if there was no room to move, at least nothing could sneak up behind me.

Tucking myself into a small ball, I maneuvered under the large root, shuffling down until my eyes were almost level with the ground, tucked away in what I hoped was a safe space.

God, I hoped it didn't rain tonight.

The winds overnight had been something I'd never

experienced before—almost tornado strength but without the whirlwind, only a constant single-direction gust of cold wind that chilled me to my bones and beyond. I tucked further into myself and eventually got to sleep, probably more from sheer exhaustion than any level of warmth and comfort.

When I woke, I found my robe had been tucked around the parts of me exposed outside the roots. This sent me flying from partially groggy into full-blown alarm in a matter of seconds. I kicked off the robe and scrambled from underneath the roots, looking around wildly for any sign of life.

Nothing.

"Who's there?" I called, and when there was no answer, I picked up my robe and waved it by my side, soil and leaves falling from it. "I know someone is there. You gave me my robe back."

There was movement, and when I shifted my gaze to the spot I swore I had seen something, there was nothing apart from the unanswering forest. I took a step forward, tilting my head before stopping again. "Is someone there? Can you help me?"

When I took another step, there was an audible crack as a branch broke, possibly underneath a foot. I swooped down and scooped up another fallen branch, holding it like a bat again, my robe forgotten at my feet. I'd managed to kill one thing by blindly swinging a stick, so I might as well keep to what works.

Until it doesn't.

Because whatever this was, it was a hell of a lot bigger than the beaver thing.

There were eyes, bright green and blazing between two trees. It blinked at me, and I stared back, trying to figure out how I could decide if this creature was friend or foe without simply waiting to see if it tried to kill me.

My jaw dropped as the creature stepped out into the light, and I took a step backward. It was around seven feet tall and huge, like *fucking huge.* Its skin was the same deep green as the forest floor with vines that twisted around its body, some of which had tiny pale pink flowers growing out of them. Lifting my eyes to meet the creature's gaze, it looked almost human. Like it *could* be human if its skin was different and it wasn't so ridiculously big. Long, thick, deep purple hair was braided, trailing over its shoulders and down its back, some of which were twisted into some of the vines that appeared to be part of its body.

Did I mention it was carrying a massive fucking spear?

I took another step backward, and the alien watched me. It pointed at my robe on the ground. "Ackta." Its voice was a rumble but had a soft tone to it. In some ways, it was so humanlike it threw me. I took another sweep of its body—same number of limbs as me, four fingers and a thumb curled around the spear, and *it…fuck.* Scratch that… *he* had a massive fucking erection as he watched me.

Not good.

When I stepped backward again, he pointed again to the robe. "Ackta."

"Whatever you say, buddy." I held up my hands in surrender, although my fingers were still curled around the stick I was wielding. I slowly bent without taking my eyes from him, scooping up my robe and slinging it over my shoulder. He lifted the corner of his mouth, almost into a smile, and I frowned. Okay, so me having my robe back made him happy. Did that mean he was the one who took it? Not necessarily. He could have found it or seen what had taken it and came to return it to me.

I guess I should say thank you.

But I couldn't find the words. My mouth was dry from shock and a sudden realization I hadn't had anything to drink in almost a day.

I shuddered, and with the alien man still watching me, I very slowly put on the robe, not wanting to lose it again. I'd need it to protect me from those winds at night. The alien continued to stare, his eyes on every movement I made, widening slightly as each of my hands popped out the sleeves in turn. Did it not know what clothes were? He was naked, so very fucking naked, and once I noticed, it was hard to stop my eyes from darting down to his crotch, where his impressive cock was on full display.

When I looked at his face again, he appeared almost smug, and my cheeks flamed. *Better not stroke the alien's ego, lest he get the wrong idea.*

The spear was concerning me. Apart from the size of the alien himself, the spear could be thrown. If he ran toward me, I might have a chance to escape. I was half his size and could probably duck and weave between the roots and get away. But if he threw a giant weapon at me? Not a chance.

Yet he just stood there, watching me.

"Can you understand me?" I asked, figuring I might as well test the waters here. He eyed me for a moment longer, then broke into a large smile. It was near impossible to resist smiling back—he just looked so damn pleased with himself. I guess it was kind of cute. "Okay." I took half a step forward, never taking my eyes off the alien man. "How about we start with something simpler? Do you have a name?"

He released a string of gibberish that didn't help me at all. "All right, cool, cool. Um... your name, though?" Another blank stare. I pointed at my chest. "Tori." Then I indicated him, "You are?"

More gibberish but definitely the word *ackta* was in there somewhere, and once again, another grin and a point at my robe. Damn, he was super fucking proud of returning that to me. I nodded. "Yes, yes, very good. You brought me back my robe."

I lifted the corner of the garment. "Rooobe."

He stared at me, and I stared back.

Moments passed.

"Robe," I repeated.

There was the smallest flicker of a smile on his lips, then he muttered, "Ackta."

My lips twitched in frustration, but when I watched his face, I got the distinct feeling he was fucking with me. Almost like he knew *exactly* what I was trying to say and decided instead to play silly games. His eyes were bright and full of life, curiosity, and a cheeky spark. Too much so for him to be some big dumb animal. It looked like I'd finally encountered intelligent life on this planet.

If only I could communicate with him.

"What is your *name?*" I tried again, pointing to myself, giving my name again, and then asking him.

"Vitri."

"Ah!" I threw my hands up. "Fucking finally. Vitri, congratulations, I'm now a thousand years old."

I knew I shouldn't be frustrated with the alien. For all I knew, he was genuinely trying, but I couldn't shake the feeling he was messing with me on purpose. Vitri continued to stare at me to the point where discomfort crawled across my skin, and the urge to get away from the giant forest alien overtook any need to continue any conversation. Self-preservation was taking over, and he watched me as though I were something to study. The images of the aliens on the ship rushed through my mind, and I shuddered. I didn't need to be prodded and probed again.

"Um, well..." I shuffled one foot before taking an experimental step back. He didn't react. "Good to meet you, I guess, random alien dude. Thanks for my... ackta. Bye."

I turned to walk away, casting uncertain glances over my shoulder. He was still there, watching me, and I gripped my makeshift bat as I moved away. There was mostly silence, punctuated only by the strange background noises of the forest. I was just about at the point where my shoulders could relax when there was the thundering of heavy footsteps behind me as Vitri raced to catch up.

When I turned, weapon held at the ready, he froze, and I frowned at him. He knew I could see him—we made pointed eye contact—but he still froze like this was a game. I had no idea what to make of the intelligence of this being. Was he an animal? Like a child? Or was he intelligent and sentient and just trying to fuck with me?

I turned again and took a few experimental steps. Clear as day, the sounds of Vitri behind me, following, pounded through the undergrowth. When I turned, he froze, holding my eye contact. His lip twitched.

We played this game for a while.

I kept moving, and he kept following, again

freezing every time I turned around to face him. Eventually, I tired of the game and stopped outright, placed a hand on my hip, and stood and stared, waiting for him to make a move. I was never very good at staring contests, and my patience was running too thin anyway. If he were intelligent, either he could help me or he couldn't.

"What do you want?" I demanded.

But Vitri said nothing, only watching me with that grin. My stomach grumbled, and I glanced down at it. The reminder I had only eaten once yesterday, coupled with the fact I hadn't drunk anything in way too long caught up with me, and Vitri's presence became secondary to this more urgent problem.

Perhaps he could be useful.

"Do you know where I can find water?" He tilted his head, and I mimed drinking from a cup, then rubbed my throat. "Water. Thirst. Oh *holy shit!*" I ducked as he came thundering toward me, putting on a burst of speed I hadn't expected. Holding my hands over my head as he moved swiftly past me, the ground shuddered with each step he took. I looked up when the sound stopped, and Vitri was a handful of steps ahead of me, watching me and smiling. He pointed ahead, and I stood, taking a few cautious steps toward him, which he seemed delighted about. He pointed again, then at me.

Because yes, of course, rushing toward me at full

speed apparently meant *please follow me, tiny stranger!*

When he was satisfied I would follow, he kept moving, ducking and weaving between the trees and shrubbery when I expected him to simply barge through them. Vitri moved with surprising grace for his size, and I almost forgot my thirst for a moment, lost in the trance of his movements. Beyond his appearance, it seemed he really was one with this forest, knowing every nook, tree, and root, and almost danced around them as I scrambled to keep up and not fall flat on my face in the process.

He stopped underneath a large tree, a single tall trunk with no branches anywhere within reach. The bark was brown but had a strange yellow tinge to it that made my lip curl in distaste. Vitri pointed happily at the tree, and I cautiously approached. Upon closer inspection, I saw trickles of liquid sliding down between the heavily creviced bark. When I simply watched the tree, looking between Vitri and it, he pointed again, and when I did nothing, he kneeled and pressed his lips against the tree. Fascinated, I watched as his tongue darted out and guided the water into his mouth. His tongue was almost a gray color and had a curve in it that he used to create a funnel and channel the water directly down his throat.

"No fucking way," I muttered. He was built for the forest. I wasn't an idiot. Evolution wasn't news to me, but it never ceased to amaze me how creatures adapted to their environments over millennia, their bodies and habits changing to the smallest detail. I craned my neck, trying to see the top of the tree but couldn't. I could only assume it somehow collected rainwater, but then again, this was an alien planet. For all I knew, this damn tree *generated* water.

Vitri stopped drinking and looked at me expectantly, and when I didn't move, he grabbed the back of my head and guided me toward the tree trunk. But he was strong, and my instinct was to resist the motion. Unfortunately, this resulted in my face slamming into the bark and a strip of it cutting my lip. Vitri released a strangled cry and let me go before immediately grabbing at me again with both hands and trying to draw me closer.

"Don't touch me," I cried, trying to keep the tears of frustration and pain at bay as my lip throbbed. Touching my fingers to my face, they came away red and wet with my blood. "Bullshit, absolute fucking bullshit." Vitri was watching me, his eyes wide and sorrowful. When he reached for me again, I slapped his hand away. "I said don't touch me!"

He withdrew his hand, eyeing where I had struck him before returning to gaze at me. He was crouched down, so now he was looking up at me— those big green doe eyes made it hard to be mad at him. Sighing heavily, I wiped at my lip before facing the tree again and gently leaned forward. I had to purse my lips and find a crevice the right size, but I was surprised at the steady flow of the water once I found it. It was more than a trickle, and although the blood from my lip mingled with the water, giving the taste a metallic sting along with the earthy flavor it already held, I was able to quench my thirst.

When I finally pulled away, Vitri was still watching me.

"Okay, so maybe you're useful to have around."

I don't think I've ever been in such a one-sided conversation, and the hulking great alien, now on his knees, looked at me with those bright green eyes. He reached up, his long fingers embellished with blunt, dark claws, and I flinched as he touched my lip.

"Bada," he muttered.

"It's okay." I could only assume he was apologizing. Maybe he was saying *mmm… blood, yum-yum, yum-yum,* but I think if there was ever a time to attempt to be optimistic, this was probably it. Standing, I took a step away from him. Tapping on the tree, I pointed in the direction I had been headed. "Are these trees throughout the forest?"

He mimicked my motion, pointing from the tree, and then swept his arm around the forest. I took that as an affirmative. "Right, thanks." I continued the way I had been heading. Vitri was useful, but he was also *very* touchy, and I wasn't okay with that at the best of times, let alone with an alien I wasn't entirely convinced wasn't trying to fatten me up to eat me.

So, I started walking.

Because one direction was just as good as another at this point.

CHAPTER
6

VITRI

Tori was bleeding, and it was my fault. I stayed on my knees, watching her disappear into the forest, slowly stepping over and around the obstacles on the ground. I wouldn't leave her alone. She was still too fragile, and while she had some fight in her, she needed me, even if she didn't know it. The pain I had experienced in my chest when I had injured her crushed me. The anger in her tone, even if I didn't understand the words, cut me deeper until I wished I could take away the pain and blood and experience it myself rather than have anything hurt her. The last thing I wanted to do was harm her, but I forgot my strength, and I thought she didn't understand how to drink the water.

Now, she probably hated me.

That might be for the best. She needed to forge her own life here. She wouldn't be able to make it back to her home planet, though I'm certain she would try to find a way, and maybe sink into despair when she eventually figured out it was impossible. But as long as she was safe from the Ghaal, then I would be satisfied.

Maybe these urges that had been building in the pit of my stomach since I had first laid eyes on her and caught her scent on the wind would ease with distance from her.

Only once I knew she was safe, of course.

Despite my hatred of the Ghaal, I would never escape that they were my creators, and as a synthetic organism, designed for breeding. There were elements to my DNA I could never break free from. The pull I felt toward Tori was strong, and I simply couldn't keep my eyes from her. When I had touched a finger to the blood on her lip, she was so incredibly soft, her lips offering little resistance to my touch. Then something had stirred inside me, sharp and strong, and my urge had been to claim her then and there. I had caught her looking at my cock more than once, and the visual of pressing her against the soft forest floor and penetrating her was a difficult one to shake.

Snarling, I swiped my hand across the ground, lifting a handful of loose leaves. The motion did little to nothing to ease my irritation, but sitting here, now that I had touched her, was not something I could sustain without distraction.

These urges, this animalistic part of me that drove me to breed—to fuck—hadn't been ignited in many years. I'd come across a lot of female species. But Tori, not only was I certain she was compatible with me, but she was feisty, and I liked how she hid that behind a small and fragile body.

I wanted to take her.

But I was better than that. I was stronger than the animal part of me, and with self-control and the reminder that I needed to care for her and nothing more, I could overcome the part of my DNA that drove me to reproduce.

I was sure of it.

Pretty sure.

After a while, I got up and followed Tori again, keeping my steps silent and blending in with the forest around me. I was a part of this environment as much as it was now a part of me. Adaptive and learning in nature, my skin and appearance had changed, and now I moved as one with my surroundings. If I stilled, I could blend into the forest, and Tori wouldn't know I was following her.

Simply to make sure she stayed safe, of course.

Tori stopped to drink several times throughout the day, but she ate nothing, and as the day wore on, she pulled her clothing tighter around her, slowing down and eventually stopping to find a place to sleep for the night.

An entire day spent walking and without food, she would be starving and greatly weakened. Tori had already proven she could kill to eat, so I didn't understand why she didn't do it again. She had also passed several edible plants, and only fear of further anger from her kept me from crying out and pointing them out to her. She would have no way of knowing what was safe and what wasn't or how to prepare them, and I guessed it was smart of her not to go around eating random plants.

By the time she curled into a ball under a root, I had made up my mind.

Regardless of whether she feared or hated me, I needed to teach her how to survive. I was impressed with how tough she was, but she was still a stranger here. I could go weeks without eating solid food, having adapted to photosynthesize in small doses as I changed to be part of the forest. In response, small flowers would grow on the vines that settled around my arms, originating from my spine, and it had become a habit to absentmindedly pick them off and discard them. It caused me no pain, and they were basically a waste product from my body anyway.

Tori fell asleep quickly from exhaustion, I assumed, and anger bubbled in my stomach. She needed someone to care for her. Why didn't she stay with me when I had proved I could take care of her? Instead, she had wandered off alone, preferring to take her chances by herself than stay near me. Surely, she understood when I had injured her, it had been an accident.

Stalking off, I gathered a small selection of plants she should be okay to eat and returned to leave them where she would find them in the morning, sitting and crossing my legs to watch her sleep.

If I were to teach her to survive, I would need to be able to communicate with her.

Tori had cried out at me when I had tried to touch her earlier and slapped my hand away. Even that touch ignited need in me, but in order to learn her language, I had to touch her and meld with her mind. Adaptive learning is something I could do to all living creatures if they would allow me close enough for long enough.

She was sleeping now. It seemed an invasion to do this while she wasn't aware, but I had no choice.

Moving around the roots, I settled into a crouch near where she slept. Her breathing was shallow, and I frowned again. She had allowed herself to become malnourished. There was no way I was leaving her alone now. Tori could hate me all she wanted. I would care for her, and maybe one day she would realize I was only trying to help.

Maybe one day she would open her legs and welcome me to mate with her.

Snarling quietly, I shook the thought from my mind.

I was better than that.

Slowly, I released my vines, and they unwrapped from my body and reached toward Tori, sliding around her body and holding her still—one of them laid across her eyes in case she woke up in a panic. As selfish as it may be, I didn't want her to associate me with fear any more than she already did, and it made me sick to blindfold her, knowing she'd be frightened if she woke, but I couldn't stand the idea of her looking at me as though I were a monster.

Tentatively, I reached out and placed two fingers and my thumb against her temple. She stirred but didn't wake, and after a moment, I closed my eyes and joined with her mind. Her language was not complicated, but a surprising number of physical gestures went with it, and beyond that, an entirely new level of language devoted entirely to sayings, innuendos, and acronyms.

She stirred, murmuring in her sleep, and I pulled my hand away from her head, alarmed. I dared not wake her. I thought I had more than enough of her language to communicate with her. I didn't want to put her mind through too much in one go.

My vines slowly eased away from her body and

lowered her back to the ground. She still slept, but it wasn't a peaceful sleep anymore. Her brows knitted together, and she twitched and fretted in her slumber.

Standing and frowning with guilt settling in my stomach at the knowledge that I had interrupted her sleep, I returned to my home. The first sunlight was hours away, and I'm certain I could make it home and back with some supplies for her before she woke.

Then I would need to find a way to tell her I had invaded her mind in order to communicate with her and hope she didn't hate me more than she already did.

I shook my head rapidly as I walked as if to shake the thoughts from my mind. It shouldn't *matter* if she liked me or not, that was irrelevant. What was important was that she was safe, could fend for herself, and learned which parts of the island not to go to. Her feelings toward me didn't matter, and regardless of the stirring in my crotch at the thoughts of her soft skin and scent, I needed to push all that back down where it belonged. Because I had the same duty as my brothers—to protect misplaced species—and that was what I would devote my life to. I glanced down at my body, my nudity had seemed to bother her earlier, and it hadn't escaped my attention the multiple layers she wore to cover herself up. Maybe this was a cultural thing. Maybe one day she'd let me ask her about it.

While at home, I would fashion a quick covering for my genitals so as not to bother her further.

I would do anything to make her like me, and no matter how much I tried to shift the thought, I couldn't. Because stirring inside me, like sparks coming to life after years in a dormant shadow, was the need to claim beyond the need to protect.

To possess.

To mate.

CHAPTER
7

TORI

Strange dreams had interrupted my sleep last night, and when I woke, I gripped my head as it throbbed slightly. It wasn't so much pain as an overt awareness, and I lay for a moment with my eyes closed until it eased. I had dreamed of books, words and numbers, memories and people—things that flashed across my vision too quickly for me to get a good look at them. But it gave me a headache.

Maybe the air on this planet was slowly poisoning me.

There's that good old-fashioned optimism again.

From where I lay, the sunlight dappled through the forest's canopy, and the constant background noise of creatures was a dull murmur as the day began. It was beautiful, and if I were home, it would almost be peaceful. The forest, aside from the blanket of deep green, was full of odd flowers and plants of incredibly vibrant colors that made the earth's flora look dull and boring by comparison. Winding up a tree opposite my current hidey hole was an almost black vine that broke off into brilliant orange and purple flowers, opening up and exposing pollen centers of bright red.

Crawling out of my spot, I shook the excess soil from my hair and clothes. My hair was beginning to bother me. I would need to find a way to cut it off so I didn't have to deal with it. Despite my love for creating unique and personalized hairstyles for other people, I didn't care much for my own, and I'd have shaved it off if my manager had let me. She said people wouldn't trust a bald hairdresser. I wanted to call bullshit, but instead, I forced a smile and agreed.

Some of the stone I had used to build the fire on the other night was almost slate-like. If I could break off a shard and sharpen it somehow, perhaps I could hack most of my hair off and keep it out of my face.

My stomach grumbled as I straightened, and I clutched it, still slightly bruised from the aliens' assault on the ship. Yesterday as I walked, I had cursed myself for not asking that damn forest alien man what I could eat in this place. I'd walked past several plants that resembled fruit, but how could I know? I didn't fancy hunting for every single meal, but today, I may be left with no choice. If I let myself grow too weak, I wouldn't be much use against a threat.

Coming out into the open, I almost tripped over a small pile of what looked like fruits and vegetables, apparently left intentionally where I would find them. Frowning, I crouched down, finding also a small skin bag filled with water and a spear that looked to be the right height for me.

"Vitri?" I called, standing, and held my hand above my eyes as I gazed into the shadows. There was no answer. Was he still following me? Or had he come across me last night and decided to leave some food? Either way, I was grateful. Sitting, I picked up the nearest thing. It looked almost like a pear, but its skin was oddly textured like fish scales. After giving it a sniff, I took a tentative bite. The fruit exploded with juice inside my mouth, so much that it ran down my chin and over my lap. The inside of the fruit was almost like jelly, and it began to spill out. Instinctively, I lifted it and sucked the contents into my mouth. Oddly, it tasted like a sweet cheese, and I hummed as I ate because all I was thinking of in this moment was what other tastes I might encounter with this feast Vitri had left me. A pang of guilt stabbed at my chest as I ate because I had dismissed him quite quickly when it appeared he really had wanted to help me. He was playful in an annoying kind of way, but he hadn't tried to hurt me.

Except when he slammed my face into the tree.

I touched my lip. It was a bit tender, but it had stopped bleeding. I think I could safely assume it was an accident, and he simply thought I hadn't understood how to get to the water.

It would have been nice to have some company, even if the conversation was one-sided.

There as a rustle of foliage from the trees in front of me, and I paused midway through another piece of fruit—this one purple to match the flowers I had seen, and bitter, but not so much so I couldn't tolerate it—and picked up the spear to my side.

Coming to my knees, I called out, "Vitri?"

There was no answer, but the rustling continued. I stood and held my spear to the ready, just in case it wasn't my friendly forest alien or another of his kind but something more sinister.

The air was knocked from my lungs as I was tackled from the side and thrown to the ground, my spear forced from my grip and tossed out of my reach. I managed to roll onto my back as the creature came down on top of me. She was tall and slender, with long limbs that flailed about as she restrained me. Naked, I could see her small breasts, all six of them, and her skin was a deep red, dappled like a seashell and rough to the touch. I tried to grab her arms as she straddled me, trying to pin me down and bellowing at me, the sounds like an angry bird to match her beak-like mouth. Her wild black hair fell around her face and over mine—hair that led to patches of fur that covered the top half of her arms and what looked like most of her back and thighs. She kept screaming at me, her black eyes glassy, and I tried to fight even as another one stepped out from where I had heard the rustling and gathered what was left of my food in her arms before disappearing back into the forest.

"You *bitch,*" I said through gritted teeth and managed to land a punch on the alien woman on top of me. She bellowed again and placed a hand on my forehead, gripping with her claws and lifted before she slammed my head hard against the ground. I saw stars but continued to fight her off. Next, she went for my robe, pulling and yanking at it until I was forced to roll onto my stomach while it was taken from me. When she tried to steal my pants, I lost it, kicking out at her and landing a foot to the side of her face. She recoiled and hissed at me, showing a line of tiny, pointed yellow teeth before snatching up my robe and disappearing into the forest after her friend.

Breathing a sigh of relief, I moved to push myself

up, taking a moment to rub the back of my head and check my body for blood. There was none.

I was barely on my feet when I was again slammed into the ground. She was back on top of me, now wearing my robe and grabbing at my hair, pulling my head back.

When there was a deep roar from ahead of us, the alien woman and I looked up. She released my hair and stood, glancing between where the sound had come from and my pants before fleeing again. Wasting no time, I was on my feet, ignoring the need to sway as my head throbbed, and raced to grab my spear in time to spin around and meet whatever fresh hell this forest was serving up to me now.

Vitri burst through the foliage, his expression such raw rage that I stepped back. His eyes flashed with anger as he surveyed the area around me, taking in the mess of whatever food was left, my partially shredded pajama pants, and finally me, covered in dirt and wielding a spear.

He roared something, a single syllable with a series of clicks after as he looked wildly around again. With his impressive chest still heaving, he approached me as I stood frozen on the spot, barely aware I was trembling. Vitri was radiating danger, and despite his gifts and previous care, he was an unknown and could be as reliable as a wildcat for all I knew. When he was level with me, he gently pried my fingers from the spear, and although I initially resisted, I eventually relented and let him take it and drop it on the ground next to him. Vitri then traced his hands over my arms, glancing at my face intermittently with concern before dropping to his knees and repeating the motion on my legs.

Holy fucking shit. I think he was checking me for injuries.

Who *was* this guy?

I couldn't stop shaking. For some reason, despite this being an alien forest on a strange planet, I'd felt almost *safe* here, like my little routine was enough to protect me from unknowns. Foolish, I knew. The one creature other than Vitri I'd encountered I managed to kill and use for food, and I hadn't come across anything that seemed a threat to me. The pretty sounds and colors had lured me into a false sense of security, and the appearance of the banshee women had shaken me more than I'd like to admit.

Vitri started making a soothing purring sound that was borderline a growl emanating from his chest. I clenched my hands into fists at my sides because it wasn't fear, adrenaline, or shock that was making me shake anymore.

Once I calmed from the attack and took a few deep breaths, I realized it was *him.*

Because this close, Vitri smelled incredible, like nothing I've ever experienced before. It was masculine and earthy with a hint of spice, and with him kneeling in front of me, it was nothing short of intoxicating, washing over me on the cool, slight breeze that I was now wishing was an ice-cold shower. I wanted to touch him or at least steady myself on his shoulders as he continued his inspection of my body. He was so physically imposing I wouldn't have thought he was even capable of such a gentle touch, but his fingers danced across my skin, pressing at intervals to make sure I hadn't been injured. I allowed myself to take in another deep breath, and my head almost spun with the lure of his scent. I'd managed to time it so poorly it was the exact moment he pressed his palms to my thighs where my pajama pants were ripped, and I shuddered. His hands felt amazing on my body, and for the first time since landing on this fucking planet, I felt truly safe. Even having had the dangers so abruptly and thoroughly rubbed in my face, I felt safe with Vitri.

And possibly I felt horny, but I was choosing to ignore that part.

Vitri was a lot of things, but it really seemed as if all he wanted to do was care for me. For whatever reason, he wanted to help.

And how could I say no? I think I'd done all right so far, but how long could I keep this up without a guide to teach me about this planet? How long would I have to walk before I came across another alien? Perhaps one that was from a civilization capable of space travel? I had no way of knowing if they even existed. Maybe Vitri and his forest alien family, wherever they were, were the most intelligent beings on this planet. I didn't know if I'd survive long enough to find the other girls. I'd be no good to them dead.

"Ackta," Vitri mumbled, running his fingers along my arms, bringing me crashing back into the moment and making me shudder again. He still smelled amazing, and it was with desperation and willpower that I didn't touch him back.

Get a hold of yourself, Tori. He's an alien.

"Yes," I whispered, barely able to manage anything louder. "My robe is gone. Those alien women took it." He frowned and stuck a finger in one of the tears on my pants, tugging at the fabric. "Yep..." my voice shook as he looked at my face, level with mine, as he straightened his back while he remained kneeling. "Guess I'll need to find a way to make new clothes."

As he nodded, I frowned.

Did he understand me?

Could he understand me all along?

"Vitri?" He looked up, those bright green eyes boring into mine. He still hadn't stopped touching me, his hands never ceasing their movements over my body. He wasn't groping me or catching a feel, although his hands brushed across the underside of my breasts at one point, and part of me wished he would linger. When I took a shuddering breath, he shuffled closer on his knees, and after a pause where he offered me a questioning look, he placed his hands on my lower back. I had no choice but to hold onto his shoulders as he yanked me gently closer to him, inhaling deeply, his lips close to my stomach. I cleared my throat, trying desperately to clear my head too. I think I'd done an all right job of keeping my shit together since I got here, but in his embrace, I felt vulnerable and weak, like all I needed was a hug.

And a hug from a tender giant alien was as good as any right now.

But beyond that, I wanted more, and the combination of feeling secure with him, of the sheer masculinity of his body despite its odd color and texture, and his scent were making me want more—things I definitely shouldn't be thinking about with an *alien.*

God, imagine explaining that one to the other girls when I eventually found them.

"Vitri," I said again, and without breaking eye contact, he ran his hands down from my back and over my ass, cupping me and pulling me against him. I gasped. "If you don't stop touching me like that, I'm going to do something I regret."

Comfort. I needed comfort. That's all.

I was lost in more ways than one.

He was here, and I was here.

And this was crazy, but I *needed* Vitri.

Leaning forward slowly, I stopped when my lips were a whisper away from his. Closing my eyes, I pressed my lips against his and kissed him gently before pulling away. He was frowning at me. "A kiss," I said, lifting my hand to touch his face but hesitating before making contact. "Do you not know kiss?"

Oh my God, what was wrong with me? Why was this turning me on so much? Images of his cock I'd seen yesterday flashed in my mind, and I looked down to find he'd covered himself with a loin cloth of sorts. Whatever animal he'd used to create it had a deep, teal-colored skin.

Did he do that for me? That's kind of sweet in a weird alien way.

Hey, I like you, so I covered my cock from your view. How romantic.

I moved in to kiss him again and traced my tongue along his lips. Vitri jerked away from me, studying my face before leaning back to me, I guess giving me permission to keep going, and watching me with a frown as I complied. When he opened his mouth, I put the tip of my tongue against his, feeling the curl of the muscle. His entire body jerked, and his hands grabbed me almost painfully. He kneeled there, with his lips slightly parted, looking at me expectantly as if to say *do it again.*

I did, and this time when I pressed my tongue to

his, I massaged it gently. He groaned a deep rumble that moved through his chest and ended in a growl. Suddenly, his hand was on the back of my head, and he had driven his tongue into my mouth— exploring, tasting, and licking. I gasped and whined, flexing my fingers against his shoulders and pushing slightly to try to calm him down.

The growling in his chest increased to a steady purr, his hands grabbing and sliding over my body, up to my shoulders and down my back before squeezing my ass again. I could feel his chest heaving against me, and I started to worry. He was getting much too worked up over a kiss.

With a groan, he grabbed the sides of my pants and yanked them down.

I pulled from the kiss. "Whoa, whoa, slow down there. It was just a kiss." His eyes were blazing as he brought a hand between my legs, flashing with lust when I grabbed his wrist. "No, Vitri. *No.*" He stopped moving and watched me again with an expression I couldn't read. "Do you understand 'no'? No touching me there." I had to fight to pull away from him, and after a moment, he finally released me.

As I pulled my pants up and took a handful of steps away, Vitri stayed on his knees, a slight frown creasing his forehead and a very large erection lifting his loin cloth. Fuck, what an idiotic thing to do. I'd allowed my emotions to get the better of me. I was in a vulnerable position even being on this planet, and it was foolish to allow myself to be in any position even more at risk.

Like being fucked by some giant forest alien.

"Fuck," I muttered, running a hand through my hair and groaning in frustration when I hit a handful of knots. "Fucking bullshit. Fucking *fuck.*"

Vitri watched me as I began pacing across the spongey forest floor. I needed action. I was restless and needed anything to get the feeling of his hands on my body out of my mind.

I spun around to face him. "Vitri, I need to cut my hair." He kept looking at me, so I held out a lock of my hair and mimed chopping it with my hand. "Hair, I need to cut. I need a blade or anything sharp." He watched me for a beat longer before standing, and with one last look back at me, he moved into the forest and disappeared from view.

CHAPTER 8

VITRI

Tori wanted to cut her hair, and I didn't understand why. Was this some sort of mating ritual? She hadn't told me.

But I would help her regardless.

Because Tori had finally let me touch her—really touch and *feel* her in a way that stirred desire in me in a tightening coil threatening to release. At first, I was simply checking for injuries after she was attacked by the Turnk females—a gathering and collecting species who were too wild to reason with, more victims of the Ghaal's search for compatible mates—but then Tori had become aroused. Her scent was strong in the air, and it intoxicated me to the point where my head was swimming and my control was slipping, and that was before she touched her lips to mine. It was a delicate touch that reminded me how soft her lips were, as if I needed reminding it wasn't something plaguing my mind every second. Tori had touched her mouth to mine—a kiss—and then her hot and wet tongue had pressed against mine, and the coil holding me together began to unravel.

I wanted to show her what else I could do with my tongue. I wanted to taste her sweet cunt and lap up all her juices.

Holding my hands up in front of my face now, I scowled at the tremors that passed through my fingers—a sign of weakness as I struggled to keep control of an instinct I had mostly forgotten. A part of me I had kept hidden under my skin for so long I had deluded myself into believing I was in complete control of myself. There had been many females dumped on this planet, but Tori was the first and *only* one to bring out this arousal in me. When she let me touch her, instinct stirred stronger than before, and my original pure intentions were wiped from my mind, replaced with depraved thoughts of mating her.

Fucking her.

But then, she pushed away, and then she was

angry again. I didn't understand why. I had simply continued what she had started, and her ripped clothing was only a barrier between my hands, mouth, cock, and her absolute pleasure. She said *no*, and, of course, I understood it, although I couldn't tell her that. Not now.

I couldn't simply ask her why she was angry and stopped me. Tori was already mad, and it didn't seem like a good time to tell her I had melded with her mind while she slept. An intimate act I had undertaken, again with good intentions, but ultimately without her permission. I was also angry at myself because had I waited one more night—a matter of *hours* even—I would've been able to touch her mind this morning while she was awake and aware of it. I could've explained to her what I was doing and why, and then she wouldn't be angry.

Maybe then she wouldn't have said no, and my cock would be sunk deep inside her wet heat by now.

Too late for that.

I would find Tori a sharpened stone to cut her hair and even help her if she wanted me to. Anything to settle down her fiery spirit so I could reveal to her I knew her language, understood her, and could speak to her too. I'd like to know where she was going with such determination, walking as if she had a mission to complete. Considering she was on a strange planet, I could certainly help her.

If she'd let me.

If I could contain my instinct and keep my hands to myself.

I had blades I'd fashioned from bone back in the home I'd built amongst the treetops, but I didn't want to leave Tori alone for that long, so I simply found the flattest stone I could and sharpened it against another, hoping it would be enough to do as she wished. Her hair was silky smooth and finer than mine, and I suspected the sharpened stone would easily slice through it.

When I returned, Tori was sitting cross-legged near the large roots she had slept under, and she stood as I approached, brushing herself off and waiting for me, her eyebrow cocked and hands on her hips. I stopped a few feet from her, and the smell of her arousal was still in the air, and her shredded clothes did nothing to disguise it. Unable to hold back the groan that escaped my lips, Tori lifted her other eyebrow at me before glancing at the stone I held and holding her hand out expectantly.

When I didn't hand it over immediately, she thrust her hand harder between us and said, "Hand it over. Thank you." Her tone was terse and clipped, and it didn't improve when I clutched the sharpened stone to my chest and pointed at myself.

Both her eyebrows rose further at my gesture. "You want to do it?" She pressed her lips into a thin line, her foot tapping as she studied me. "I dunno about this, Vitri. You're still an alien to me, and for all I know, you're going to use that stone to slice my neck open." She dragged her finger along her throat and made a choking sound to emphasize the motion, and my eyes widened. *Did she really think I would hurt her?* "Of course…" she continued, now playing with her hair, "… you can't even understand me, can you? So none of these musings will do you any good."

My jaw clenched as she continued to study me. Every second I waited to tell her I could understand her stretched out and increased the betrayal, making the ultimate acknowledgment more painful. Should I just chime in with something? Would there be a perfect moment to reveal what I had done? Uncertain, I chose to remain silent. Maybe I could get her to let me touch her mind and then pretend I hadn't done it the night before.

The idea sprung a sharp pain in my chest—it was painful to deceive her. My indecision continued to plague me, but as I opened my mouth to respond, she moved forward and closed the gap between us before pressing her palms to my chest. I couldn't help the rumble of satisfaction that moved through my body and the spike of heat and pheromones I couldn't contain, pushing all other thoughts of a confession from my mind. Because Tori was near me, who I wanted to claim as my own, to bring pleasure and have her delicate body pressed against mine. She hummed gently with me, rubbing her hands on my chest for a moment and smiling as my growl of pleasure increased in volume before holding one hand out, palm up. "Vitri…" she purred out, her fingers still tracing lines across my chest, "… please hand me the stone."

I did because I apparently had no control when it came to denying her wishes.

She went to move away again, and I growled, wrapping my arms around her. The realization she had only touched me like that to get her way stung a little, but she also thought she was still in a life-or-death situation, and since I had betrayed her first, I could forgive her for the lie.

My lips lifted into a smirk. If she wanted to play games with me, then we could play.

Tori wasn't struggling but staring hard into my eyes as though she could get her way this time by simply glaring at me. Her little bouts of anger were starting to come across as cute, given how harmless she appeared to be, so I simply smiled at her. She smiled back, but it didn't reach her eyes. Keeping the stone firmly grasped in one hand, she placed the other on my upper arm, stroking it as she had done my chest earlier.

"Let me go, Vitri," she murmured, impatience flashing in her eyes despite her smile and cool tone. "I have a feeling you understand me more than you're letting on, so I'm asking you nicely to let me go."

"Kiss," I mumbled, and her eyes widened, the smile dropping from her lips.

"I'm sorry?"

"Kiss," I repeated.

Tori's gaze was firmly on mine, and I felt her body slacken slightly as her arousal increased, the scent almost bringing me to my knees. "Are you suggesting that if I kiss you, you'll let me go?" She bristled at the implication, but something in her eyes told me she was not only considering it but wanted it too. This brought on another surge of possessiveness that flared in my chest.

If she wanted me back, I don't know if I could contain myself.

I only watched her and loosened my grip on her slightly. She still didn't move, and when I released her entirely, she stayed standing right next to me, her breasts pushing against my stomach. We stood like that for a long moment, and as a shudder ran down her spine, I traced my fingers down her arm's smooth skin.

Content with having turned the tables on her, I took a step back. I had no intention of forcing her to do anything for any gain of my own. I had vowed to watch and protect her and that I would. But she liked me more than she was letting on. Despite our differences, there was an attraction there, and my cock throbbed with need at the revelation. If Tori would only stop being so stubborn and give herself to me, I could show her worlds of pleasure.

And simply hope I could keep control of my instinct as I did.

What if once wasn't enough?

Tori cleared her throat and stared at the stone in her hand, turning it over in her palm before running her finger tentatively toward the sharp edge. She looked impressed, and I grinned as she glanced up at me, quirking a brow before glaring at the smug satisfaction on my face.

"Okay, so I'm impressed you could find something suitable so quickly. Good work." Her lips lifted into an almost smirk as I continued to grin at her, and then she looked around before back at me. "Actually, I could use your help since I'm now one hundred percent convinced you understand me. See that flat stone over there?" My gaze flickered to it just long enough for her to understand I had registered, then I looked back at her because I never tired of staring at her. "I'm going to lay my hair out over it, and I want you to chop it off so it's nice and short, okay?"

She handed me the stone, and I accepted it, following her to the area she had indicated. Tori draped herself near the edge of the rock and lay her hair delicately over it. As instructed, I used the sharpened stone to cut her hair. It went through easily, but her hair kept moving, and the cuts were uneven. She kept replacing her hair on the stone, and I kept cutting until she was satisfied. Tori stood, running her fingers through her new short hair and humming. "No more knots," she said, flicking her head around a bit. "For now, at least. Thank you."

She approached me again, and I smirked. Cutting her hair had brought it from midway down her back to up near her ears, and her dark hair sat at odd angles where I hadn't cut it evenly. It was messy and wild, and I loved it. Tori pressed her body against mine again, and I stiffened. What game was she playing now? I'd done as she wanted, and she still touched me. My mind whirled as I tried to understand her motivations. I'd fed her, brought her water and a weapon, saved her, cut her hair, and still, she touched me.

She took one of my braids in her fingers and twirled it. "Vitri," she breathed out the word, and a growl rumbled through my chest at the sound of my name from her throat. "I know you can understand me. You can tell me how you did it. I promise I won't be mad."

I hesitated, but the warmth of her body was testing my control. Tori was writhing against me, moving to a beat or sound I couldn't hear but didn't need to. She was so delicate and warm, and a shudder ran up my spine as I placed my hands on her hips. She didn't move away, and I released a slow breath. She was almost dancing with her slow swaying, taunting, and teasing me, and my eyelids fluttered closed for a moment as I tried to regain control, my fingers tightening on her hips.

"Vitri," she whispered again in a pleasant sing-song voice that she coupled with more tracings of her fingers along my chest in small circles, her skin in contrast against the green of mine. "You can tell me."

This had to be a trap, but I couldn't resist. She purred my name again, and I growled.

"I can understand you," I said finally.

Tori shoved away from me, slamming her palms into my chest and pushing. "I fucking *knew it!* How long have you understood me? How long have you been able to talk? You better tell me what the fuck is going on before I *lose it!*"

I didn't know what she was going to lose, but the rage was ebbing from her, and despite her being half my size, I took a step back, ground she quickly regained by taking another step forward.

She said she wouldn't be mad.

I guess she won this game.

CHAPTER 9

TORI

With a hand on my hip and my foot tapping, I waited for an explanation from Vitri, and it better be a damn good one. It was a chore to keep my breathing steady, but simply the *idea* that there had been life on this fucking planet that could understand me and could've been able to help, and yet he said *nothing* drove me crazy. And to think I let him *touch* me the way he did, that I touched him back, that I *kissed* him. Touching him hadn't been unpleasant. In fact, it had been almost pleasurable. His skin was like soft leather, and he responded to every touch, no matter how delicate. The rumble deep in his chest, somewhere between a purr and a growl, only left me wanting more.

And the scent. God, he smelled so fucking good.

But he had *lied* to me, and none of the rest mattered now.

When Vitri didn't say anything, I lost control of my inner thoughts, and they spilled out of me. I yelled at him, adding in a good measure of obscenities and *bullshit* to emphasize my point. At least he had the grace to look bashful at what he had done as my rant faded when I was going around in circles, repeating myself, trying to abate my anger over lost time I'd spent wandering when I needed help.

But he did *help you,* my inner voice whispered, and I silenced it with another string of muttered curses.

"Well?" I finally demanded after I'd had my say, and he still hadn't responded.

"Tori—"

"Yes, that's something I know you can say. So how about you use all the other words you know, and while you're at it, tell me how long you've understood me?"

"Only today," he said, his voice slightly gravelly. *Good,* I hope he felt bad.

"How?"

Vitri fidgeted uncomfortably, shifting his weight

from one foot to the other, and the vines that wrapped around his body twitched and shifted with the movement. The sight of a seven-foot alien being caught in a lie and acting like a scolded child was almost comical. "I got your language from you."

I prodded him in the chest with my finger, and while he watched the movement, he didn't step back. "Listen here, buddy, if you've used some bullshit alien mind reader on me, you better have a damn good explanation."

His eyes widened, and I swear I had to fight the urge to laugh. Surely, he was aware that physically, I was no match for him. He was practically cowering, and damn if it wasn't almost *sweet.* But I shook the thought from my mind as he responded. "I'm not sure what you mean, but I didn't use mind-reader technology on you as such. I used my own abilities. My learning is adaptive, and I can learn languages through connecting with another's mind."

"And you did this to me *when?*"

Another uncomfortable shift from him. "As you slept."

He opened his mouth to speak again, and I held up a hand to silence him, closing my eyes for a moment and taking a few deep breaths. Despite my anger, I didn't know how far his patience would extend if I continued screaming at him. He was, after all, twice my size. "Let me get this straight," I said, balling my hand into a fist and bringing it to my side, slowly opening my eyes before holding his eye contact. "You followed me after we parted ways yesterday, then when I was asleep, you read my mind to learn my language and then spent all morning *not* telling me you could understand me?"

His eyes darted about as if looking for help, and again, I almost laughed. "Yes."

"Vitri." I placed a palm flat on his chest, and if possible, he looked even more alarmed than he had a moment before. What did he think I was going to do to him? I knew what he *hoped* I would do to him, but he seemed switched on enough to realize that wasn't about to happen. "You do understand how incredibly fucked up that is, right? Or are our cultures that different that reading someone's mind while they sleep is just a totally okay thing to do here?"

"I understand it was wrong, and I'm sorry. I only wanted to help you, and you weren't letting me get close enough to get your language. But then you let me touch you this morning… and I realized if I had waited a few hours, I could have done it with your permission. But by then, it was too late, and I didn't know how to tell you."

Okay, so I guess that made sense.

"Are you afraid of me?" I asked. His bright eyes were still wide, and he hadn't moved away nor made any move to get me out of his personal space.

A slight frown creased his forehead. "I'm afraid of disappointing you. I only want to help."

"Why?" He said nothing and looked around again. I flicked his chest with my fingernail to get his attention. I would have flicked his nipple if he had any. "*Why do you want to help me?*"

"Can we please sit down? I have a lot to tell you."

"Fucking right, you do."

Vitri frowned again. "You use that word a lot and often out of context."

"What? Fuck?"

My eyebrows shot up as he trembled slightly before answering. "Yes."

I sighed. "It's just how I talk, Vitri. It releases tension for me. It's called swearing."

"You must be very tense."

I eyed him, unsure if he was messing with me or being serious. The slightest twitch of his lip gave him away, and I almost smiled. *Almost.*

"I think I have reason to be, don't you agree?" Vitri only nodded and sunk to the ground on the spot, patting his knee. I chuckled, but it was hollow. "I'm not going to sit on your lap." I sat opposite him, tucking my legs underneath me so as not to expose myself by being cross-legged in front of him, given the fact my pants had no fabric to cover my crotch, thanks to my asshole abductors. "Spill. Tell me everything."

"My creators still live on this planet—"

"Whoa, don't just glaze over something like that... your *creators?* Like, you're a cyborg?" I glanced around, searching between the trees before looking up. "Or are there literal *gods* on this planet?" I mean, I had no way of knowing the kind of power that existed in the far reaches of the galaxies—it was technically possible. Weren't almost all things technically possible? The idea thrilled and terrified me. On one hand, super-powerful beings were a scary thought, but on the other, they could get me home.

But Vitri shot down my epic fantasies with his answer, which was, granted, fascinating in itself. "I'm a synthetic organism. I breathe, eat, live, and die. I'm alive in every sense, but I was created in a lab, engineered for a purpose."

"What purpose?"

"If you'll let me explain for more than seven words at a time, I'll tell you."

My jaw dropped, but he had that damn smirk plastered on his face again, and I couldn't stop my lips from lifting into a small smile. "All right, fine... tell me your story. I'll be quiet."

"My creators, the Ghaal, were a dying species brought to the brink of extinction by their own violent nature. The result of chemical warfare left the remaining numbers with fertility issues. Most of the Ghaal left the planet to search for somewhere else to inhabit, and they took the knowledge of most of their technology with them. Since their departure, nature has flourished, taking back the areas the Ghaal no longer occupy."

Then Vitri looked grim and pressed his lips together in a thin line before he continued, "Those remaining created my kind, the Synths. Six of us in total. The Ghaal, despite their advancement, are superstitious about the number six. We were designed to learn and adapt to our environment, physically..." he held his arms wide, and my vision swept over his green skin and the vines, "... as well as enhanced learning abilities." Vitri pressed a thumb and forefinger to his head before holding his hand in the space between us. "And, of course, to breed with enhanced libidos, attraction pheromones, and the ability to change genders." Vitri sighed, and I frowned, wondering how long it had been since he'd told this story. "What the Ghaal didn't count on was that my brothers and I would see them for what they were, and in the end, we would refuse to help and turn our backs on the colony. They are a violent race and not worth saving if they cannot learn to treat themselves and others better."

He paused and closed his eyes tightly. I touched his knee, and Vitri's eyes shot open. He stared at me with such intensity that an entire world of emotions played across his features I couldn't begin to imagine. "Why am I here?" I asked, and he closed his eyes again, and panic and dread settled in my stomach. "You know, don't you? You know why I'm here. That's why you're trying so hard to look after me."

"The Ghaal became desperate after being cut off from intergalactic trade—no one is to leave or arrive on this planet anymore. They employed the assistance of another species, the Moeks, to help. The Moeks are also dwindling in numbers, but unlike the Ghaal, they are mostly peaceful. The deal is this—the Moeks search the galaxies for potentially suitable life forms to breed with. If they do not suit the Moeks, they dump them here for the Ghaal to try in exchange for food and fuel, both abundantly available here."

My stomach dropped, and I made an involuntary choking sound I couldn't cover—for the Ghaal to *try* like we were disposable. "On the ship..." I piped up, and Vitri looked at me with sad eyes, "... they probed the other girls and me, but when they cut my clothes off..." I shuddered, and Vitri made a low moaning sound, "... they didn't seem to like what they saw, and they dropped us here."

"The Moeks will not proceed if they have to hurt you or do anything surgical. The Ghaal, on the other hand..." he swallowed, rubbing his hand over his face, "... the Ghaal will do anything necessary to ensure the continuation of their race. But you..." he paused again, and I wondered what could be so difficult he couldn't tell me, given the truth bombs he'd already dropped. "You are the species they've been hoping for. You're in danger here… they want you."

I closed my eyes for a moment, taking this all in. Being used to breed wasn't a scenario I hadn't considered while we were on the Moek's ship—I'd seen horror movies and read books—but confirming out loud was something else. When I opened my eyes, Vitri was still watching me, his green eyes blazing with intensity, a brighter version of the forest that surrounded us.

"So…" I sighed out, trying to remain levelheaded enough to absorb all this information, "… where do you come into all of this?"

"My brothers and I separated, and we live around the island. When the units are dropped from the Moek ship, we try to track them down, communicate if we can, and teach the new species to survive on the planet. Sometimes we can't communicate, so at the very least, we attempt to guide them away from the Ghaal colony by the mountains and keep as many as we can safe. We may not always succeed, and I'm starting to suspect the Ghaal are creating camps to get to the units before we do, but we will keep trying."

"Wait, so those batshit crazy ladies with the bright red skin who attacked me…"

"They were kidnapped from their home planet

and dropped here. They are wild and difficult to communicate with. They wouldn't have killed you, but they are collectors and often try to rob new arrivals."

"Good to know," I muttered, drawing my arms around myself, suddenly unable to get the chill from my body. "Speaking of which, I need new clothes."

"I can make you some."

Lifting my head to study Vitri, he still watched me with that intense look. The scent of him washed over me as the direction of the breeze changed, and I shuddered. He still smelled amazing, and I remembered what he said about his pheromones. I'd need to remind myself not to get sucked in by him, no matter how much I wanted to touch him. He was my only stability on this planet, and now finding out that there were other aliens here who would try to find me, kidnap me again, and use me to breed made me want to vomit. My stomach churned in agreement with my fear.

"Tori," Vitri whispered, and I pulled myself from my thoughts to look back at him. "I will keep you safe."

"Why?" The word was barely a whisper—a single breath that shuddered as I held in the emotion that threatened to overtake me—because all this information was too much.

He looked at me like he could see right through me. "Because I know you're in more danger than the others. Your similarities to me and the Ghaal, the way I felt when I…" he shook his head, "… they will want you." His eyes swept my body, lingering between my legs. "I will keep you safe because you deserve better than what has happened and because…"

"Because?" I prompted.

"Because you make me happy."

I squeezed my eyes closed again, shaking my head. "That makes no sense. You don't even know me."

"You're vulnerable here, and I've touched your mind. Perhaps I know you better than you realize."

I didn't need to hear this. "I need some space. I need to think." Vitri stood as I did, and when I went to move away, he gripped my arm and pulled me back. His skin was smooth and warm against mine, and all I wanted to do was melt into his hold. I couldn't get the memories of how he had touched me and our shared kiss out of my mind.

But that's not what I needed right now.

I needed to be alone, to think and sort out my thoughts.

I needed to pull myself together before I fell apart.

"Vitri, please…"

"I will let you have time but let me make you some clothes first. I promise it won't take long."

"I want to try and find the other girls."

"I'll take you back to my home, make you some clothes, and you can even bathe if you like. Then you can have some time alone to think. But know this..." Vitri drew me closer, his arm around my waist, pulling me against him so my breasts pressed against his hard stomach. "I won't be far behind you. I know this forest. I have been here for a long time, but something is different these past cycles, and I feel the Ghaal are closer than I realize. They will know you're here, and I will not let you from my sight. I was foolish not to come to you straightaway and walk by your side, but I won't make the same mistake again. I will protect you, Tori."

I shuddered at his touch and, for a moment, I allowed myself to sink into his hold before I pulled away and indicated for him to show me the way to his home.

He made me want to stay with him and forget about everything else.

But I couldn't, without purpose and something to do, and left alone with my thoughts for too long, I feared I would lose my mind.

CHAPTER
10

TORI

The journey back to Vitri's home took hours, and I wanted to protest, but I struggled to keep my thoughts coherent. Everything Vitri had told me swirled around in my mind, and it didn't help that he continually glanced back at me as we walked, concern etched into his features. I set my expression into stone, wanting to be unreadable to him, but even so, my eyes would mist up occasionally, and I wouldn't be able to hide it in time before he glanced back again. He went to say something a handful of times but stopped before making a sound after I shot him a look that clearly portrayed *I don't want to talk about it.*

The second I opened my mouth to confront my reality, the tears would start, and I wouldn't be able to stop them. I hated crying.

Along the way, we stopped a few times to eat a selection of plants that Vitri chose, pointing out which parts were safe and edible and which were not. We'd drink from the trees as he had shown me the previous day, and I'd been able to get him to leave me alone only long enough to squat behind a tree for a moment of privacy to relieve myself.

The forest changed, and the large roots that dove in and out of the ground surrounded by the bright flowers and vines were replaced with thinner trees, still of the deep, earthly green but ascending into the sky for at least ten feet before the first branches appeared. Just when I thought I would run out of energy, Vitri stopped by a cluster of trees that looked no different from the rest. I didn't want to stop again until we got there, and my shoulders slumped with the effort to keep awake. Another break and I just might not be able to get back up, and I certainly wasn't going to let him carry me.

Vitri nudged me, and when I glanced up at his face, it was adorned with his gorgeous grin. I pressed my lips together in a vague attempt to return the smile I couldn't find the energy for. Then he pointed up, and my jaw dropped.

He lived in a fucking tree house.

It wasn't elaborate, but it didn't need to be. It was simply a well-disguised platform amongst the higher branches, made from intertwining strips of wood. It had walls and a roof and looked like it would be well protected against the winds at night. One of the supporting trees was the type that provided water, so he would have a constant supply in his home.

"My God, Vitri," I breathed out the words, everything else momentarily forgotten. "It's beautiful."

His chest literally swelled with pride at my words, and with agility that surprised me for his size, he leaped at a nearby rope, and the muscles in his arms worked as he pulled himself upward. He then waggled the rope around in front of my face, and I balked.

"You're kidding, right? I can't climb a rope." Flashbacks to gym class haunted my mind, and *that* rope had knots it in. This was just a rope, a vine even, tied to a tree with no means to get any foothold. When there was a chuckle from the treetop, I glared at him.

"Next time, I'll carry you then," he yelled, seeming to take great joy in the idea he would need to carry me up and down to his home. "But this time, just grab on."

I muttered a string of obscenities, wound the

rope around my wrist and palm, and held on with both hands for dear life. I couldn't contain the squeak of alarm as I was jolted upward before Vitri began a steady pull on the vine, lifting me to his home. Repeating the mantra of *don't look down* in my mind did nothing, and when I, of course, looked down, I moaned. It looked so much higher from the elevated vantage point.

Stumbling onto the platform, I grabbed Vitri's arm to steady myself, trying to bite back a squeak of fear that threatened to escape. This section had no barriers, and I felt exposed and vulnerable. He chuckled again, allowing me to keep a vice-like grip on his arm until we were inside the treehouse and he had pulled the door closed behind him. I let go and moved across the floor, marveling at how cozy it appeared. The water tree was in the corner, and the steady stream of the clear liquid created dapples of movement in the light as it trickled down and out of sight beyond the floor. There was a large pile of what appeared to be teal animal skin and furs in one corner and a selection of spears and weapons in another.

The floor creaked as Vitri moved toward me, and I squealed again, clinging onto the nearest beam. "It's sturdy, right?"

In response, Vitri simply chuckled and began jumping up and down on the platform. I screamed at him to stop, not finding it even half as amusing as he evidently did. The tree house shuddered, ominous creaking adding to Vitri's laughter at my discomfort. But it didn't budge, crack, or even bow, and Vitri was still laughing as he came to a stop and pulled me against him. The deep rumble of his laughter through his chest vibrated against my ear, and he held me as my breathing slowed and my heart stopped threatening to burst free from my chest—images of plummeting to the ground still vivid in my mind.

"That wasn't funny!" I cried as I pulled away.

Vitri smirked again. "Yes, it was."

I huffed out an unimpressed breath and moved to find a place to sit. Vitri made his way over to the pile of furs and began pulling out pieces, holding them in front of himself and either discarding them back into the pile or putting them aside.

Exhaustion began to take over, and I sunk to the floor, my back against a supporting beam. "You said there was somewhere for me to bathe?" I asked.

Vitri nodded, his smile hesitant as he gazed at me. "There is, but I don't think you'll like it very much. It's on the roof."

"On the *roof?*"

"Rest. I'll make you clothes. Tomorrow, you bathe, then I'll give you time to think."

I nodded, curled up into a ball, and whispered a thank you when Vitri draped a fur over me.

I wasn't even sure I wanted time alone to think

anymore.

I think I just wanted to stay right here.

Either I was more exhausted than I thought, which I put down to emotional and mental overload, or Vitri's tree house really did keep the winds out. Or both. Because I slept the rest of the day and all night, waking up in the morning only when Vitri shook me gently awake and handed me a water bag to drink from.

"Would you like to bathe before you try on your new clothes?"

I sat up, the fur that had been draped over me fell to the floor, and I rubbed my eyes with the ball of my palms. "Yeah, that would be nice."

Vitri nodded, and his grin returned as he helped me to my feet, moved me into the center of the tree house and pulled open a trapdoor in the ceiling. I swore as his hands found my hips, hoisted me up without prior warning, and waited for me to grab the edge and haul myself onto the roof. I gripped the panels of wood, finding fingerholds easily in how they were weaved together and clung on as Vitri pushed me through the opening. As I waited for him to pull himself up, I breathed a sigh of relief that there was a small fence-like barrier around the roof.

"How long did it take you to build this place?"

Vitri shrugged. "It's been so long, I don't remember exactly. I did it over several seasons. Adding to it as needs arose."

That told me nothing. How many seasons did this planet have? How long did they last? I still had so many questions.

Before I could ask them, Vitri ushered me to one of the corners and determined not to look down, I kept my gaze plastered straight ahead.

"Whoa…" I muttered.

From this height, I could see over the tops of the trees with the large roots in the distance. The sun was steadily rising. The difference of the light from the orange star cast a breathtaking glow over the distant ocean, then spread out across the land unfolding beneath it as the light appeared bit by breathtaking bit. I could see the mountains in the far distance and shuddered as I remembered the Ghaal colony was around there. But there were fields and forests spread out to both sides, and beyond that were rivers disappearing into the distance. The ocean was a dirty gray that looked like dishwater, but it still made me long for Earth. I'd never been much of a beach person, but the horizon with the waves dappling the sunlight bouncing off the water looked so strikingly familiar

I wanted to go there.

But it also appeared so far away.

"It's beautiful, isn't it?" Vitri came up behind me, snaking an arm around my waist and pulling me against him. I rested my palms on his arm but didn't push him away. Instead, I tilted against him and let the steady drum of his heartbeat and roll of his breathing lull me to relax. I almost forgot how high we were and that we were standing on a structure made only from woven wood.

I sighed and pushed away from Vitri, who released me after a beat, the reluctance to put distance between us heavy in his movements.

"So, how do we do this?"

Vitri pointed up, and I followed his indication. At the top of the water tree were large shell-shaped leaves of a pale pink, and I could see the water shimmering in them in the rising sunlight.

"Don't we drink that water?"

"Don't worry. The rains come regularly, and we'll use only one lot to bathe in. There are plenty of others to keep us refreshed with water until the rains return."

I nodded, trusting his judgment, and when I lowered my gaze from the giant leaves, Vitri had removed his loin cloth, his cock hanging down the inside of his thigh, almost as thick flaccid as it was erect. I stuttered for a few moments, then pulled my gaze away, staring determinedly at the tree trunk as if it were the most fascinating thing I'd ever seen. "Wh-what are you doing?"

"What's wrong? Do you bathe clothed on your planet?"

My cheeks flamed, and I hated that I was embarrassed. "No."

Vitri simply cocked an eyebrow at me, and anger flared behind my embarrassment. "Fine," I said, pulling my top over my head and lowering what was left of my pajama pants, I dropped them both to the side. I stared at Vitri as if challenging him to say something, but he simply gazed over my naked body, not at all ashamed of looking, and when I realized he was erect, I tried and failed to keep my focus on his eyes.

"You can look if you like," he said, chuckling, moving his hips slightly from side to side, making his cock bounce with the motion. He grinned as my eyes widened. "I'm looking at you."

"I noticed."

"You can touch me if you want."

Heat swelled between my legs at the seduction in his tone. His cock twitched as I watched it, and I'd be lying if I said I didn't want to drop to my knees and taste it or feel what it would be like to be stretched by him.

I cleared my throat. "I think we'll just bathe today."

Vitri smirked and handed me a large white

flower. The pollen spores inside the petals were rounded and large, and following Vitri's lead, I squished them between my palms, amazed when they burst into a frothy substance. I bit my lip against a moan of delight as I washed away days of grime using the froth and decided I wouldn't bother hiding that I was watching Vitri do the same. The lines of his chest, arms, and thighs were enticing, even if his skin was an odd color. When I raised my gaze, his eyes were boring into mine, flashing with lust and hunger. I tried desperately to ignore the feeling his look gave me as I continued to lather myself, running the suds through my hair and eventually pulling my gaze from his.

"Ready?" he asked.

"Ready for wh... fucking *bullshit!*"

Vitri had prodded the bottom of the water tree's leaf with a stick, causing the entire amount to overflow over the edges and dump unceremoniously over us. The water was cold, and I screamed in alarm as it hit my skin, its sheer volume and force enough to wash the suds from my hair and body.

Vitri shook his head and body like an animal, the vines that were part of him unwinding from his arms and torso and shaking before returning to their place. I shook my head, splashing him with water.

"What the fuck was that?" I cried, shivering. The

romance of the moment stunned me the second the icy water had been dumped on my head.

"Bathing." Vitri shook again to rid himself of the water I'd splashed on him. "You're clean, are you not?"

"I'm fucking cold and wet, is what I am."

"And clean," Vitri added, smiling. He held out a hand, and with a scoff, I took it and allowed him to help me back into the tree house.

These clothes he made better be fucking warm.

CHAPTER
II

VITRI

With the furs, I had fashioned Tori a tunic that wrapped around her body and tied at the side and a pair of boots she could slip on to protect her delicate feet and calves. Although I hadn't heard her complain on our journey here, her feet shouldn't be bare. She was too fragile and needed to be protected. I also made her a cloak to keep her warm, but I don't think she'd need it yet. Despite the winds at night, this was the warmer of the seasons, pleasant and sunny during the day.

I had been playful with her this morning. A small

smile had played on her lips, but it would vanish the moment I stopped joking around, and she would disappear again into her thoughts. We'd dressed, and Tori clung to my neck as we descended from my home—tree house, she called it, and I liked that. The heat of her body against my back was soothing, and again, my instinct stirred. I wanted to carry her somewhere where I could lay her down and penetrate her.

She was quiet as my feet landed on the ground, and she slid off my back with a muttered "Thank you" and stood for a moment, twisting her hands together as if unsure what to do.

"Go," I prompted, pointing into the forest. "Have your think. You'll be safe, and I won't be far away."

She looked at me, her eyes wide and calculating. There was a hint of fear there, and I wasn't sure if my presence was a comfort to her or not. I hoped it was. I wouldn't hurt her.

As we walked, I slowly fell behind, allowing Tori to get as far ahead as possible while still being in my sight. If she had noticed this, she said nothing and remained locked within her mind. My chest ached for her, and I tried my best to understand. I had left my home by choice, but Tori had been taken and abandoned on a new planet, left to survive for herself. She was at risk of being taken again the second her feet had touched the ground, and now, thanks to me, that fear danced in her mind too. But

I *had* to tell her. She needed to know why she was here and that she must be cautious. I couldn't allow her to be taken by the Ghaal.

I *wouldn't* let it happen.

Every few moments, I would let her slip from my sight, wanting to give her the privacy she needed, but the panic would overwhelm me, and I would take a few rushed steps to make sure she was okay. Not once did she turn around to face me, but simply kept her head bowed as she ducked and weaved amongst the vines and roots. So, I slowly let her get further ahead until I was relying only on the sound of her walking. Feeling emboldened and sympathetic to her needs, I allowed even that to drown out. But it was too much—I needed to at least hear her. My desire for her still stirred within me, and deep down, I wondered if I had enough control to keep myself in line without some physical connection to her.

Tori needed this time alone, and the least I could do would be to offer it to her.

Her footsteps stopped, and I assumed she had sat down, taking a moment to compose herself. I ached because she was hurting, but there wasn't anything I could do to make that go away. She needed to mentally work her way through her situation, and then I could help her build a life here.

Because there was no going back to her planet.

I was drawn to full alert when I heard a scuffle

and gripped my spear as Tori cried out, "*Vitri!*"

She was calling for me.

My female called for me.

I was already on my way before the word had completely left her lips, having not let her get too far from me. She was safe with me, and I would never let her stray even this far again.

When I burst between two trees, Tori was on the ground, pinned down by a being twice her size. A roar of rage escaped me as I launched at the being, shouldered him in the ribs, and knocked him off Tori. She screamed and rolled out from under us as we struggled, and when he grabbed my wrists, my vines snaked out from my back and wrapped around his arms, ready to throw him.

"Vitri, it's me, Ilk."

I recognized him but, in that moment, the anger was still burning strong in me. No one was to touch Tori except me, and no one was to hurt her. Period. This had gone beyond my duty to protect the displaced species. Tori had awakened the long-dormant part of me designed for breeding, connection to my brothers, and seeking a mate.

Ilk.

Reaching deep inside myself for whatever small iota of willpower I could find, I drew on it, controlling my anger.

My brother.

I didn't want to kill him. I knew that.

I held my breath, at least for a moment, so I couldn't smell the scent of Tori's fear, a scent that drove me crazy with the need to protect. Stopping my vines from progressing as they snaked around Ilk's torso, I looked into my brother's eyes— another Synth I had not seen in many years. I'd forgotten exactly how long it had been.

"Ilk?"

I shook my head slightly, realizing I still had him pinned to the ground, and as I stood, I held out a hand to help my brother up. He was incredibly heavy, and I took a moment to take in his appearance. Ilk had taken up home near the foot of the mountains as close to the Ghaal colony as we dared to get and living in the mountains had changed him as much as living in the forest had changed me. Like the rocks, his skin was dappled gray and purple, and he was hard as stone itself. His features were flat and sharpened around the jaw and nose, but we still shared the same green eyes.

"Rock boy," I muttered, barely able to contain the smirk that grew on my lips. I gazed at my hands and then at Ilk's. Bred to adapt, I had never seen it in practice to such an extent. Before this, we lived together and all looked the same. To know what differences our environments could make us, I wondered about our other brothers across the island. Would I even recognize them now? Would the oceans, rivers, and woods have changed them so much they were no more than strangers to me?

Tori came up to my side, jabbing me hard in the ribs with her finger. "What are you doing? This ass attacked me. I thought you wanted to protect me, and you're just letting him go?"

I moved to grab her and hold her around her waist, but she frowned at me and sidestepped my swipe. With a grin, the vines from my back lashed out and wound around her wrists and torso, spinning her toward me until she was against my side. Ilk watched with an expression I couldn't read as Tori cried out in anger, struggling against the grip of the vines, which I released the second I scooped her next to me with an arm around her waist.

As I knew she would, Tori didn't give up and began beating at my chest with her palms. Still angry from the attack, she stilled for a moment as I introduced her to my brother and Ilk to her.

My feisty female was still angry.

"That's fucking fantastic. Let me *go!*" she cried after the introductions. I released her with another chuckle and let her move out of my grasp. Tori lifted her spear or at least half of it—it must have been damaged in the scuffle with Ilk. Using the dull end, she prodded Ilk in the chest in what I thought was a bold move—a part of what I liked about her so much.

"What do you know about Erica? What have you

done with her?"

I frowned. "Who is Erica?"

"Another human woman," Ilk said, his expression shifting again. "The Ghaal took her in this forest. We came looking for you," he added, looking at Tori as if this was somehow her fault. "They must have camps set up, waiting for the units before we can steer the species away. Erica is my mate, Vitri. We have to get her back."

"Your *mate?*" Tori whispered and spared a moment to glance at me. I held her gaze for as long as she would let me, remembering the feel of her under my hands and wishing to have her again. If the female—Erica—had let Ilk claim her, then maybe eventually Tori would take me as her mate. I'm certain Tori was sharing the same mental images as me as we glanced at each other, and I wondered if she knew the pleasure I could bring her. The spark that had ignited when I first touched her flared to life with hope she may one day be mine. My muscles tensed as I had to fight for control again, and I turned to Ilk as Tori asked, "What makes her your mate?"

"I claimed her."

When Tori looked at me, her eyes widened as if realizing the implications of Ilk's words, and I smirked. Her friend had mated with Ilk, so maybe Tori would realize the attraction between us wasn't so crazy and give in to it rather than fighting so hard. I tried to communicate this to her without words, my fingers twitching with the need to reach out, pull her toward me, and take her right here.

The moment was shattered by a roar from Ilk. "Are you going to help or not?"

"Of course, I'll help, then we can find the other humans. Yes?"

Tori threw her arms up. "That's what I've been saying!"

I smirked, enjoying pushing her buttons. "Only because I said it first... an excellent idea."

Tori huffed out in frustration but said nothing else. Ilk's rage increased with every passing second, and I tried to think how I would feel if Tori were taken from me. I slapped Ilk on the back with an open palm, and his shoulders stiffened under my touch. "Can you take me to where she was abducted?"

He nodded and turned to leave. I rounded on Tori, who stopped midstep as if she were going to follow me. Unacceptable. "Go back home and wait for me."

"Ex*cuse* me?" she cried, pressing her hands to her hips and leaning forward as if trying to intimidate me. "You're not the boss of me."

I closed the gap between us and bent low to grab her shoulders, lifting her off her feet so we were face to face. Her eyes widened again, but she didn't struggle. I hoped she knew I wouldn't hurt her, but the panic and rage seething from Ilk was difficult to ignore. He was worried about his female, Erica, as he should be if the Ghaal had her. I couldn't stand the idea of Tori being taken as well. The thought alone shredded me inside.

I couldn't go back to being alone now that I knew what it was to have her with me.

If she let me claim her, I'd never let her go again.

"The Ghaal are dangerous, Tori, and despite what you think of me, I care for you and your well-being. I will help save your friend, but please, *go home*."

She searched my face, uncertainty, determination, then finally understanding crossed over her eyes before she nodded. When I placed her gently back on her feet and turned, I stopped when she reached out, touched my arm, and twisted my vines around her fingers to make sure she had my attention. Her hand was so warm I was flushed with thoughts of holding her still with my vines while I fucked her.

This was not the time to be having such thoughts, but with Tori, I couldn't help it.

"Be careful," she whispered, gripping my arm. "Okay?"

I touched her face, a gentle touch that had her eyes fluttering closed for a moment. "I will. Wait for me."

I didn't want to leave her, but I needed to help my brother.

CHAPTER 12

TORI

Vitri and his strange brother, who I wasn't a fan of, were gone for hours. The asshole had basically jumped me, grabbed at my ankles when I tried to run away, and pinned me beneath him. Vitri was built, but he wasn't made of stone like his brother apparently was.

Literal. Fucking. Stone.

It was like being trapped under an angry gargoyle, and it wasn't something I planned on reliving any time soon.

Adaptive, that's what Vitri had said. And I must

admit, I enjoyed the feel of his soft, leathery green skin a lot more than I had Ilk's stony texture. To be fair, though my introduction to him had been far from ideal, I guess if he was worried about Erica, I could cut him some slack because apparently, he'd *claimed* her.

Damn girl, fucking an alien within a few days. Bold.

My eyes shifted to the direction I had left Vitri, and I felt somewhat like a hypocrite. Not because I had fucked Vitri but because I had seriously considered it more than once. The guy riled me up and pissed me off, but he was also cheeky and funny, and damn if I wasn't physically attracted to him despite our very clear differences.

Ilk said the Ghaal had taken Erica, and the thought sent chills down my spine. I'd made it back to Vitri's home easily enough but couldn't climb the rope to true safety. Not for lack of trying, but I got as far as hanging from my arms with my feet six inches off the ground, looking and feeling ridiculous before I gave up. So, I pressed my back against the wedge in the trees and kept what was left of my spear at the ready. I took a quick break once or twice to get a drink, but every sound that came from the forest, every chirp or broken twig, was enough to set me further on edge and return to my post. *Waiting.*

The revelation the other girls and I were brought

here simply to be vessels for breeding stirred up a mixture of emotions in me that bundled together in a tight knot. So none of the emotions could get a clear path to being dealt with, I had to sit here and let them simmer, hoping that at some point, I would feel settled enough to work my way through all the bullshit going on in my head.

I was angry, afraid, and worried. I was lost, desolate, and a whole shit ton of other things that merged to create a ball of uncertainty that sat heavily in the pit of my stomach.

The realization I didn't feel this way when Vitri was around bothered me.

He was stability and safety in a world I didn't know or understand. Where around every corner was potentially something else that could harm me, or not, but the unknown was a danger in itself. The fact I didn't know more about the potential threats was as bothersome as the threats themselves. I could protect myself, but the unknown definitely got to me. I had no desire to injure or kill a creature that didn't deserve it, and what if, in fear, I lashed out at something that was simply going about its day? For all I knew, there were giant, terrifying-looking creatures on this planet that were peaceful as hell and cute and small creatures that would rip off my face. Vitri knew this place—he was such a part of this world, the vines were literally growing out of his fucking back.

And I absolutely *should not* have been excited at how he wrapped those vines around me and drew me against him like some kinky bondage game of the best kind. So, I reacted the way I always do when resenting my feelings.

Anger.

Ilk had said he had *claimed* Erica, and the idea cemented in my mind that his words could only translate to one thing—Erica had fucked that great hulking stone alien. I tried desperately not to judge her. Who knows what sort of connection the two of them had formed in the time they'd been together? What they'd been through? Lord knows Vitri was growing on me—pun not intended—despite my best efforts to ignore it. I liked to be challenged, and dammit, did that man—alien—challenge me. This entire situation did. But beyond his poking, prodding, and jokes was a fierce protective streak that absolutely should not turn me on.

But it fucking did.

I would have to pick Erica's brain about her relationship with the Synth alien, if only to ease my conscience about my conflicting feelings. Because when it came to fucking Vitri, a part of me thought *why the fuck not?* It seemed there wouldn't be a way to get home, and even if there were, we had immediate dangers and obstacles to stumble over first. So what if I wanted to feel good in that time, wrapped in the embrace of an alien whose vines made me think about what dirty things he could do with them?

I would talk to Erica.

Because Vitri and Ilk *would* find her.

My stomach began to grumble, and I ignored it, scrambling to my feet before standing at attention when I heard the approach of several beings.

"Please be Vitri, please be Vitri," I repeated under my breath, hoping he didn't have some mega-alien hearing or something. No doubt he would give me a hard time about wanting him back near me so badly. *Ha ha you missed me* or some shit.

My lip twitched. Almost a smile.

Dammit, he was growing on me.

"Tori!" There was the sound of running footsteps as my name was called out. I dropped my spear and ran to meet Erica halfway, grabbing her before she came to a complete stop, wrapping my arms around her. I wasn't usually much of a hugger, but fuck, I was *so* glad she was safe from the Ghaal.

"Oh my God, girl, it is so good to hear your voice," I said. Erica chuckled, tears streaming down her cheeks. On instinct, I ran my hands up and down her arms, maybe checking for signs of injury or to reassure myself she was real and safe. Erica seemed unharmed, and I could only hope she was okay emotionally as well as mentally. Who knows what hell the Ghaal subjected her to, even in the space of a few hours? "I mean, literally, I've only heard you speak once, and I'd forgotten what you sounded like."

She laughed again, and I pulled her against me for another hug, releasing her only when my usual discomfort at the closeness of a relative stranger ebbed through. We held hands, squeezing slightly.

"Samara?" I asked, searching Erica's face for answers about the other girls. "Misha?"

She shook her head, and my stomach sank. "I was going to ask you the same thing. Ilk and I came here first to find the nearest pod, aside from the one on the other side of the mountains." Erica threw a glance at Ilk. Her expression was weary, but she still offered him a small smile. "Ilk says he has a brother on the other side of the mountain who would've gotten to that pod."

I threw a look at Vitri, who responded with a smirk. "Lucky her." So whoever landed near the other side of the mountain would have also found an alien man to look after her? Damn, these fucking guys were everywhere. I wondered if they were all as possessive and protective as Vitri and Ilk. According to Vitri, they were designed for breeding, so perhaps it was part of their nature to be protective over females.

Erica continued, "The other pod landed near the ocean on the other side of the Ghaal colony."

A chill ran down my spine at the mention of the Ghaal. "Those fucking creeps," I spat out before running my hands up and down Erica's arms again. "Are you okay?"

"I'm okay, but I really think we need to find the others."

"Agreed."

We turned to face Ilk and Vitri, and I crossed my arms over my chest, ready for Vitri to make another smart-ass comment about how looking for the other girls was his idea all along. The jerk was still grinning at me, and we stared at each other for a beat until I lost the ability to maintain my anger at him and almost slipped a smile.

Ilk spoke up, his voice deep and gravelly, "We'll make a plan," he said and approached Erica with heavy steps and grabbed her upper arm with surprising gentleness, considering his size, before steering her away. "But I need to talk to you first."

Erica didn't object and followed Ilk into the forest until they disappeared from view.

I sunk back against the trees, and Vitri came and sat next to me. "Are you okay?"

Shuddering, I wrapped my arms around myself. "The idea that the Ghaal had her, and they could have..." I choked past the words, unable to finish the sentence. A growl rumbled through Vitri's chest, and I studied his face. I already missed the smirk he usually wore. "That means they're close, right? They could have grabbed me?"

It felt selfish to ask, but the fear clutching at me

from the inside forced the thoughts of self-preservation into my mind. While the fear had been a constant companion since I was taken, being faced with the idea of the Ghaal so close increased it into a ball of vulnerability.

Vitri stood and held his hand out to me. "Come."

"Where are we going?" I asked. Even as I took his hand, his green palm was as smooth as velvet in mine. He didn't answer, and I didn't repeat my question, instead following him through the trees, heading back behind the location of the tree house instead of away from the entrance. The forest thickened here, and Vitri moved expertly through the trees. I stuck close to him, following his path and watching only his large back in front of me. He never let go of my hand, and when the trees opened up into a clearing, I gasped. Vitri chuckled. There was a small break in the trees, creating a private nook where what was left of the day's sunlight streamed through the gaps in the treetops and highlighted the bed of flowers that grew.

I looked between them and Vitri. "These flowers look the same as the ones that grow on your vines."

Whether he did it consciously or not, Vitri picked one of the flowers from the vine that wrapped around his arms and dropped it. "All these flowers are part of the same plant, a giant root system that takes up almost the entire forest." He sighed heavily and had a dopey smile on his face that was almost cute. "It's all one being, one life form, one system, and I'm a part of that system now."

He sunk into the flower bed, and I followed suit, reluctant to squash the beauty by sitting on it, but sighing with him as I did. They were soft like feathers on a duckling, and I brushed my hands across them.

"Can I kiss you?" Vitri asked, and I held his gaze. "Why?"

His jaw tightened as he clenched it. "Erica was almost taken from my brother, and the idea of losing you…"

"Will a kiss keep me safe?" I whispered with a flicker of a grin as Vitri shifted closer to me until we were side by side.

"It will remind me that you're still here and safe with me." I released a squeak when he sharply pulled me next to him with an arm around my waist. "As long as you're with me, I'll never let anything happen to you."

"Promise?" It was childish to ask him to promise such a thing, but I leaned into his touch when his fingers brushed against my cheek. *Maybe I should let him protect me.*

"Promise."

When he reached for me, I didn't stop him, and his large hand cupped my cheek seconds before his lips found mine. The position was awkward, given our size difference, and before he got too into the kiss, I kneeled and straddled his lap, wrapping my arms around his neck and kissing him before he could put too much thought into the change of position. His tongue sought access to my mouth, and I parted my lips to play my tongue against his, moaning into his touch as his hands trailed down my back.

With a grunt, he pulled my body flush with his, and I groaned against his lips when I realized he was hard. I couldn't help it, and I began grinding my hips against his length, needing the friction against my aching clit. He hadn't made me any underwear, and his loin cloth offered no protection, slipping easily to the side so I could slide his length between my pussy lips. Vitri growled, sudden and loud, making me jump, but his fingers gripped my hips and continued rocking me across his length, the bump of the head of his cock hitting my clit, making me moan.

As we deepened the kiss, I opened my eyes, startled by the new sensation as Vitri's vines unwound themselves from his body and wrapped around my torso.

"Vitri." I gasped, and he responded only by gripping my chin and pulling me back into the kiss.

"I won't ever hurt you," he mumbled against my lips, and I nodded, allowing his tongue back into my mouth as he bound me next to him. The grip of his fingers on my hips was almost painful as he ground me against his length, and my breathing came in pants as my peak neared.

"Vitri, you need to stop, I'm going to…"

My eyes rolled back as he thrust forward, grinding his hips against mine, increasing the friction. "Do you really want me to stop, Tori? Or do you want to come on my cock?"

"Oh fuck…"

He hummed his satisfaction. "You're so sensitive, aren't you? I don't even need to penetrate you to make you come. I could have some fun with you. I could make you feel so good, but only when you want me back."

I couldn't concentrate enough to maintain the kiss. My lips stilled next to his, and he continued exploring my lips, fucking his tongue into my mouth as he sped up with the movement of my hips.

I was ready—my peak was right there.

Crying his name, I gripped his shoulders as I came, my legs trembling as I gripped his thighs between mine. His vines snaked around my torso when I collapsed against him, the strangeness of the situation lost on me in my bliss. I sighed against his shoulder, and his cock twitched underneath me.

"Vitri," I whispered, and he hummed, his fingers flexing on my hips. "Do you want to fuck me?"

He groaned again, and a loud rumble continued reverberating through his chest after the sound had disappeared. His fingers still flexed against me, and

I could've sworn it was hesitation. That confused me since I thought he wanted me. I was about to ask when he finally spoke, "I will fuck you, Tori," he muttered, dragging his tongue up from my collarbone to my cheek in one long, languid lick before grabbing the back of my head and thrusting his tongue into my mouth. "But not tonight. We have to get back to the others. I want to take my time with you." It felt like he was leaving something unsaid, his pupils blown wide with desire.

It was my turn to groan, and as Vitri chuckled, I scowled. "You're enjoying this, aren't you?"

"Having your cunt against my cock? Very much."

"I mean, the power over me, having me begging you to fuck me?"

He sat me up on him, his hands on my upper arms and his smirk gone, as he stared at me intently. My playful and grinning Vitri was gone, and something animalistic flashed behind his eyes. "I didn't hear you beg."

I shuddered. All my hesitations were gone, replaced only with need.

Vitri and Ilk had gone hunting, and I was glad. The fruits I had snacked on earlier in the day seemed so long ago, and I was desperate for a decent meal. I showed Erica how to drink water from the tree near Vitri's treehouse, and she was impressed. She was less impressed when I recounted how Vitri had slammed my face into the tree, but she still laughed.

"Misunderstandings with Earth sayings can lead to extreme results," Erica said with a smirk.

I narrowed my eyes at her. "Explain." But she only offered me a cheeky grin.

We sat together near the pile of wood we'd gathered to make a fire, waiting for Vitri and Ilk to return before we lit it. I was concerned the fire would draw out something else from the forest, but Erica just shrugged. Apparently, there wasn't much wildlife near the base of the mountains, thanks to Ilk driving them away from the Ghaal colony.

Erica stared at me, and after a moment, I said, "What is it?"

"I like your hair. It seems we had the same idea. I wanted to chop mine off the second it started getting knotty."

Erica's hair was still long and braided in a dozen separate braids, then pulled back into one thick plait. "I like your braids."

"Thank you," she said, smiling and running the plait across her palm. "Ilk did it."

"What made you not cut your hair?"

Erica chuckled. "I was going to, but when I mentioned it, Ilk made a sound like a dying whale."

She imitated the sound then, releasing a gloriously loud and mellow moan. I almost choked as I laughed, and she chuckled with me. "So, I guess he didn't want me to have short hair." She shrugged. "That's okay. I like the braids, and if it makes him happy, then bonus."

"When did he first talk to you?"

Erica pursed her lips as she thought through the days. "We managed to exchange names, then I let him do that mind meld thing."

"You *let* him do it?"

"Yeah, I mean, he did it for a second, and I figured out longer would allow us to talk. Wait..." she turned to me, frowning, "... you didn't let Vitri?"

"He did it while I slept," I grumbled. Erica looked like she was about to smirk, then stopped herself. Maybe she was going to remind me they were aliens as if I wasn't reminded every second I looked at that gorgeous hunk of a male.

Fuck, where did that thought come from?

"Ilk says he claimed you," I blurted out, and Erica released a bark of laughter.

"Did he now? I'll have to have words with him."

"Does that mean you've..." I trailed off, suddenly awkward about something that wouldn't usually bother me. How do you ask a new friend if they fucked an alien? Especially when you just got yourself off with one.

"Had sex with him?" She arched a brow at me, a

slight smirk playing on her lips.

"Yeah."

She looked at the ground, tracing small circles in the mossy undergrowth with her finger, but she was still smiling. "Yes. I had sex with Ilk. More than once."

I nodded, not sure where to go from here. There were a hundred follow-up questions I could ask, starting with what happened between them that drew her to him. But really, the most pressing question on my mind after my recent interaction with Vitri was, "What was it like?"

"Damn. You don't mess around, do you?"

I managed a smile, then most of my discomfort evaporated as I looked at Erica. We didn't know each other very well, not yet anyway, but we were bonded by our trauma, thrown together in this situation. The least I could do was talk openly with her. I didn't want to come to another planet just to develop another high school click with gossiping and bullshit. Or just to ostracize myself from most social situations as I had done at home.

Erica sighed, still smiling. She seemed unable to keep it from her face when she was talking about Ilk. "He made me feel so safe, you know? Looking after me. I guess after a certain point, I kind of thought, *fuck it.* Why the hell not? I'm not saying there wasn't conflict in my mind about it, but in the end, he was just so darn cute that he won me over."

She gazed into the forest, unable to see much farther into the shadows than me.

Cute? The guy was a literal gargoyle but each to their own, I guess.

When Erica turned back to me, she asked, "Did Vitri tell you about the pheromones?"

"Yeah, he did, among sooo many other things about this planet. Yet I feel like I don't even know a fraction about this place."

We sank into silence together for a moment before Erica continued, "Well, I learned the pheromones aren't a drug exactly, so it's not like they can make you act against your will. But when the Synths are attracted to someone, they can't help releasing them. And God, they smell *amazing.*"

So that's why Vitri smells so fucking good? I simply nodded, getting back to the important part of the conversation—the part that had me resisting the urge to rub my thighs together. "So... the sex?"

"The sex was *incredible.* He's... I mean, he's fucking *huge.* But then again, look at the size of him." When I didn't respond, she looked at me, a cheeky smile playing on her face. "Have you slept with Vitri?"

"What? No! Did he... did he tell you we had?"

"Of course not. I don't think lying is in their blood." She glanced at me as I scoffed.

Says her. Vitri didn't tell me he could understand me and let me mime like an idiot when I could've simply asked a question.

"Calm down, Tori," Erica said, misinterpreting my expression. "You asked me first." She held her hands up in mock surrender, but she was grinning.

"I mean, I want to, I think. We've touched each other." I ran my hands up and down my face, groaning. "This entire situation is ridiculous. Why am I even attracted to him? He's a fucking alien. I shouldn't even be *considering* having sex with him."

"Do you like him?"

I looked into the forest where Vitri had disappeared with Ilk earlier, barely containing my grin, and at this point not even sure why I was still trying to. "The idiot is growing on me."

"You know," Erica started, playing with the moss again. "An old friend of mine used to have a saying back home, which could be pertinent in more ways than one here."

"And what was that?"

She laughed. "Fuck it!"

We were laughing when our alien men came back to camp, and Erica kept tossing me knowing looks and smirks as we set up the fire and cooked their catches. Subtlety was evidently not her strong suit. More than once, Vitri caught the looks between us and would throw a grin at me, which I'd respond to with a glare, only smiling when he looked away, and I'm sure he knew.

We separated to sleep, Ilk insisting that finding a

crevice on ground level was safe. Looking at him, the big stone alien, I could understand why he wouldn't want to climb a tree and balance on a plank of wood. He'd probably fall right through it.

After hugging Erica goodnight, I draped my arms over Vitri's neck and held onto his back as he climbed the vine to the tree house, his movements not at all hindered by my weight.

I slept with Vitri behind me, his body wrapped around mine, his arm across my stomach. His warmth was comforting and exciting all at once, but I was still plagued with uncertainty.

Yet, as weird as it was, just as I was drifting off to sleep, his vines wrapped around me and pulled me against him. It should have been strange, but all it did was make me feel safer than ever.

CHAPTER 13

VITRI

The sun was barely over the horizon when we woke, and it didn't take long for us to get ready. Tori consented to bathing again before we left since I couldn't be sure how often we would get the chance along the way. Ilk assured me there were streams through the woodland areas we could bathe in, but I enjoyed the heavy rush of cold water that came from the canopy leaves.

Tori was not so thrilled with my method of bathing, and this time, I didn't bother to keep my laughter subdued when she stood there naked, her short hair plastered to her face and over her eyes, with only her scowl visible. When I didn't heed her warnings to stop laughing, she tackled me, running headfirst toward me and catching me around my waist. The attack was not enough to knock me from my feet, but it certainly knocked the air from my lungs and silenced my laughter at her expense. We wrestled for a while, and I held back my strength, allowing her to work out her arms as she twisted and turned. At one point, she kicked at the back of my heel, I assumed trying to get me off my feet. It wouldn't work, but I was impressed with her attempts all the same.

With a deft spin, I turned her until her back was against my chest and held her close to me, ignoring her struggles as I chuckled.

"You can't win against me, Tori," I hummed as she made a noise somewhere between amusement and a frustrated grunt and continued to struggle.

"Oh yeah? Well, I know your weakness." My brow furrowed as I couldn't think of a weakness I had that she could possibly exploit. But when she twisted her arm around her back and wrapped her small fingers around my cock, I cried out in surprise. "Mm-hmm, that's what I thought," she cooed at me, amused now she had the upper hand.

I groaned as she pumped her tiny fist over my length a few times until I ground into her touch. I spun her around, taking her shoulders in my hands and moving to kiss her. Tori brought up a hand between us, so I ended up placing my lips against her palm.

"Ah-ah-ah, we have to get going," she said in a musical voice. Letting her go, I snarled as she stepped out of my reach, my eyes blazing as I took in her naked body and smug expression. "I win," she said, moving to the center of the roof to slide back into the tree house.

"You are going to be sorry you did that," I grunted out, following her through the trap door. She laughed, and I tried to smile, but inside, my instincts were stirring, and I couldn't think of a way to warn her about teasing me without making her fear me.

We dressed and descended, meeting Ilk and Erica at the base of the trees. Erica had her own spear, much like the replacement I crafted for Tori, smaller for their size. Ilk and I were carrying water and other supplies.

"Let's go over the plan again," Erica said as we began to walk through the forest. "Ilk and I will go around the base of the mountains to find the pod that landed there. Although Ilk assures me you two have a brother there who would have helped, I still think it's best we check it out."

I exchanged a look with Ilk. While I don't doubt our brother, Lanir, would have helped whoever was in the unit that dropped, he was not known for being excessive with his compassion and may have been too harsh with the female, scaring her away.

Erica continued, looking at Tori. "You two will head around the woodlands to avoid the Ghaal colony and get access to the coast that isn't marred by cliffs." Her lips twisted in her uncertainty, and the worry was clear in her eyes. "I'm *pretty* sure I saw a pod go near the ocean or the coast, but we were moving so fast..." she trailed off, and Ilk intertwined his fingers in hers.

"It's not your fault. You were right to take note as much as you could," Ilk said.

"Right," Tori joined in, falling into step next to Erica. "I couldn't see the other pods at all with the way mine was spinning, so I'm glad at least one of us did."

Erica gave her a small smile before looking ahead as we walked. "After we've found the other girls..." she paused. I assumed to quash any uncertainty she had left. We *would* find the other females. We had to. We couldn't risk them being taken. It was imperative we knew they were safe. But at the same time, we were searching blindly in a huge landscape to check based on only a vague idea of where the units landed.

Ilk took over. "After we find them, we need to keep moving. The Ghaal will be after you with more determination than they've gone after other species since you're a match for them and, therefore, valuable. They've been waiting for you and won't give up easily. We'll separate into pairs again and keep moving."

Erica added, "Then after a few weeks..." she glanced at Ilk for reassurance, "... we'll come back together and discuss what to do next."

Ilk and I glanced at each other again. While searching for Erica, we'd briefly discussed attempting to gain some weapons to stop the Ghaal from continuing to come after our females and perhaps put a stop to their experiments for good. We were peaceful beings and didn't want to resort to violence unless they left us with no choice, but Erica, Tori, and their companions were in trouble.

Ilk had shared information that troubled me, and I'd decided not to burden Tori with it—the Ghaal knew the humans were a perfect match because they'd tested on them before.

Ilk described the state they'd found the deceased human female in all those years ago, and my stomach churned at the idea Tori was also in that danger. Now that they'd had Erica in captivity for a brief time, they'd be more determined than ever.

Their efforts to get hold of the women would ramp up now. Out of desperation and lack of compassion, they wouldn't stop until they had them.

I was troubled by the fact Erica was taken from so close to my home. While I'd been aware that perhaps they had camps across the island and away from their colony for a while now, the efficiency with which they located and took her was concerning.

They already *knew* these females were a match for them, so they were hunting more intensely than before. A desperate enemy is more dangerous. Ilk's information had been necessary but troubling. They killed the previous lot of human females during the experiments, and Tori and her friends were the replacements, ready to be used to breed.

I glanced at Tori, her lips pressed together in a thin line, staring straight ahead. I had no doubt she was thinking of her friends, and I wouldn't trouble her with this additional information. Not yet, not until we at least knew her friends were safe. She had enough to worry about without knowing the Ghaal had specifically sought out *human* females.

Mimicking Ilk, I slid my hand down Tori's arm until she offered me her hand and held her fingers between mine, squeezing slightly. She glanced up at me and gifted me a small smile, which I returned, making her cheeks flush. Adorable. Erica and Ilk held hands a lot, and now I did the same with Tori, thrilled she was allowing me to do what seemed such an intimate gesture. Something I would have to ask her about later.

Was this a human custom?

What did it mean?

But it was time to separate from Ilk and Erica.

We reached the edge of the forest without incident, and after a break and something to eat, Tori and Erica had an emotional farewell, promising to see each other again soon and wouldn't give up until they found their companions. Ilk and I nodded at each other, the determination in his expression matching mine before he set off with Erica across the fields toward the mountains.

I held Tori's hand and led her along the forest's edge. We would keep going in this direction until we could see the woodlands clearly, then we would cut across the field into the woodlands, which we could follow to the coast. A straight line would be quicker, but I wasn't going to risk Tori being anywhere near the Ghaal colony.

"We'll camp out by the forest's edge tonight before we head for the woodlands," I said.

"Whatever you say, oh brave explorer alien."

I smirked at Tori. "You know, on my planet, you're the alien."

She tapped her chin, mocking me. "Hmm, I never thought of that. But only one of us has vines growing out of our skin."

I laughed, whipping one of said vines out and spanking her ass, making her squeal and jump. "They're useful, though."

She swatted at my arm, laughing. But the laughter soon died down into brooding silence as she once again sunk into thoughts of her friends. I wasn't going to add to her concerns, so I simply squeezed her hand and let her think.

As early afternoon drew near, I offered to stop and have something to eat.

"Do we need to go hunting?" she asked.

"There is likely to be herds of gorae around, but if you don't fancy the hunt, we can find some luphers."

She shrugged. "Sure. Whatever works."

As we walked, I started kicking up the yellowish grasses. Tori let this go unmentioned for a while before she frowned and asked, "What are you doing?"

"Looking for signs of luphers."

"I thought that—" I shushed her with a light hiss and a wave of my hand, and she silenced, ducking down with me when I pulled her into a crouch. "I thought we weren't hunting," she whispered.

"Not exactly. Luphers are too stupid to run away, but they could crush us."

"Crush us?" Tori hissed through her teeth. "How much do you think we need to eat?"

I shushed her again, causing her to tut.

The luphers always hung around the border between the forest and the fields—another species that wasn't native to the planet, brought here by the Moeks, though I'm not sure what they were thinking even taking them. They shared no physical characteristics with the Ghaal, so perhaps it was another move born purely from desperation. Or maybe it was a joke, a small act of rebellion. Moeks were the only ones who would help, given the no-trade rules put on the planet by the interstellar authority. Ilk suspected the Moeks grabbed random species under the guise they could be used for breeding, simply to worm more fuel and supplies from the Ghaal.

The luphers had bred quickly, apparently through asexual means, which I had never witnessed the process of. I had no qualms about killing them occasionally for food—they were large and lumbering and ate more than their share, taking it from the smaller native species. After the chemical warfare, the native species had dropped substantially in numbers. Fewer luphers taking their food was a good thing.

I slapped a hand over Tori's mouth as she squealed when the lupher came into sight—a large yellow creature, brighter yellow than the grasses, and about up to my shoulder in height. It lumbered slowly, weaving in and out of the trees before dropping itself onto the grass with a thump and a huff from its beak.

"Vitri," Tori hissed, grabbing my arm. "That thing is as big as a fucking car. I don't think we need that much food. It's like a giant beetle."

I chuckled. "Just watch."

With the lupher settled, I lifted my spear, hurling it toward the creature. With a sure shot, the spear hit the lupher in the side of its large body.

With barely a sound from the creature, it exploded.

"What the *fuck?*" Tori screamed, standing and jumping backward to avoid the rush of goop flying toward us, spreading over everything near where the lupher had been standing. "Vitri, what the *actual fuck?*"

I scooped up a handful of the goop, what was left of the lupher, and offered it to Tori. "Eat."

She looked disgusted as I helped myself, sliding handfuls of the goop down my throat until I was full. Tori hadn't yet started eating, and I laughed at her expression.

"Just try it, will you?"

With a scowl, she scooped up a small handful and poked her tongue out to taste it, smacking her lips comically afterward. I waited, and she made an irritated humming sound before taking another mouthful.

"It tastes like..." she rolled the goop around her tongue before swallowing another serving. "A really bitter lime jelly."

"Is that a good thing?"

"It's passable. Next time, warn me before you explode a giant beetle, okay?"

I laughed. "Where's the fun in that?"

CHAPTER 14

VITRI

We made good time. Tori was stronger than I had given her credit for. Even knowing she could look after herself, I still thought I would need to slow down for her more than I did. The sun had not yet dipped below the tree line, so I decided we had time to cross the field, hunt a gorae or two along the way, and set up camp near the edge of the woodlands, ready for tomorrow.

Tori followed my instructions and was willing to learn, a look of determination plastered on her beautiful features. When we went hunting, she missed the gorae with her spear but assured me the one I had caught would be enough for both of us as she had filled up on *beetle guts*—her words—earlier.

She would make a strong mate, capable but still needing me to look after her. It was the perfect combination because I enjoyed taking care of her. The wonder with which she viewed my world reminded me of a magic I had long forgotten. Things I took for granted and saw as only ordinary were fascinating to her, and although she didn't often express it verbally, her eyes would widen and she'd gasp quietly at some of the plant life.

It really was a beautiful planet.

It would be more so if it weren't for the Ghaal, but then again, if it weren't for them, I wouldn't exist, and Tori wouldn't be here to be my mate.

I shook the thought from my head. This wasn't about Tori and me but finding her friends and making sure they were safe.

But I'd seen the looks she cast me as we walked, the way her hand squeezed mine for support when she needed to climb over something. The heat from her was excruciating, and I wanted nothing more than to sink my cock into the waiting warmth between her legs. Shuddering, I tried unsuccessfully to keep my thoughts from straying. The longer I was in her company, the harder it was becoming, and I wished I had asked Ilk how he contained his instincts when I apparently couldn't.

When we stopped, I made a fire, took a stick, and poked at the roots of a small gray plant, shifting it away from our camp.

Tori stepped forward, reaching out. "Oh, here, let me get that."

"Tori, *no!*"

She reached out to grip the plant, wrapping her fingers around the stalk, pulling it from the ground, and tossing it to the side. I ran to her, grabbing and pulling her onto my lap, ignoring her squeal of surprise as I stared intently at her hand and moved my fingers across her skin.

"What's wrong?" Her irritation had vanished, and she sounded panicked.

I took a few deep breaths to calm myself before answering. "Those plants are poisonous to the touch." Frowning, I studied her skin. She didn't have the gray dappling that showed the poison moving through her veins and toward her heart. In fact, aside from a slight red rash, her hands weren't marked at all. Her skin was delicate, and how was it the almost invisible hairs on the plant hadn't penetrated her skin but could do so to mine? "How do you feel? Do you feel hot?"

"I feel fine." She studied her hand as well. "Maybe the poison doesn't affect me. Don't forget I'm an alien... wooo." She waggled her fingers in my face, and I crushed her against me, easing my hold when she squeaked in protest.

My breathing was slowly returning to normal. Visions of watching the poison make its way to her heart and knowing I could do nothing to stop it haunted my mind. "Don't touch anything without asking me first. I can't lose you."

Her voice was muffled against my chest. "Deal, but next time something is poisonous, point it out to me rather than trying to deal with it yourself."

I nodded, sitting her next to me and preparing the fire, trying to calm my still-racing heart rate. As I worked, I kept casting glances at Tori to remind myself she was okay and the poison hadn't affected her. It was fast-acting. If it had gotten to her, she would already be dying. But she would return my glances, maybe cock an eyebrow at me or smile.

Tori was fine.

It was strange, but as she rightly pointed out, she wasn't of this planet. Things here affected her differently. I would have to be more careful with food. What if something I selected was poison to her but fine for me? There was no way of knowing without trying, so I would simply need to introduce her to things a little at a time. Once the fire was crackling, I began to remove the fur from the gorae and prepare it for cooking. The meat should be fine, and cooking would remove anything that might be harmful to her. Gorae had been fine for Erica, so they must be fine for Tori too.

"Wooo…" muttered Tori.

I threw her a glance, and she smiled at me. Was she excited for her meal? Was she still joking about being an alien on this planet? Unsure, I returned her smile and got back to work.

After a beat of silence, she did it again.

"Wooo wooo *wooo.*" This time, she waved her arms about, first in front of her and then above her head, back and forth in large sweeping motions. I paused, simply watching her, unsure what to make of her behavior.

"Are you okay?" I asked. Tori turned to me with a jerking motion, and I recoiled. Her pupils were dilated beyond natural for even this dim lighting. Dropping the gorae carcass, I grabbed Tori's shoulders. "Tori? Are you okay?"

She simply giggled, letting her head loll across her shoulders. "Sure, I'm just watching the fireflies!"

"Fire… flies?"

"The fireflies," she repeated, standing and swatting her hands through the air. "Aren't they pretty?" Her voice was high-pitched and dappled with giggles, not like the Tori I knew at all.

My gaze traveled to the discarded rubaee plant she had touched before.

The poison may not have killed her instantly, but it certainly was having some sort of effect on her.

"Tori…"

She turned back to me, smiling before holding her arms up and spinning. "The moon is so pretty here. It's like… *way* bigger than ours."

She threw her arms out to emphasize the vastness of the moon, and I nodded slowly. "I think you need to drink some water."

I choked back a protest as Tori pulled her tunic over her head, exposing her body to me and standing in only her slip-on shoes. From where she stood, she leaped toward me, landing against me. She straddled my lap as I sat with a grunt before she ran her fingers through my braids. "I think you need to drink some *me.*" With a giggle, she planted her face in the crook of my neck, trailing a line of kisses and nibbles along my skin as she moaned and writhed in my lap. My cock was responding, and the heat of her on top of me was unbearable. My hands trembled, afraid that if I tried to push her away, I would only pull her closer.

"I can't… Tori, please…" I mumbled, trying to regain my control as a very naked Tori squirmed on my lap. "Please… I can't take you like this."

She'd been sucking on my neck, drawing another groan from me, and released her hold with a pop. She pouted at me, running her hands around my neck and linking them behind my head. "I thought you *wanted* to fuck me?"

"I do… I *really* do… just—"

"Do you want me to ride you, huh? You can stay

sitting just like this if you want, and I can ride your cock." She demonstrated by bouncing in my lap, and I almost cried out in frustration.

I released a string of choice words in my native language, taking advice from Tori and trying to release my tension using language. It didn't work. My fingers gripped her hips to keep her still as she started grinding against me. My cock was achingly hard, and Tori was practically dancing on my lap. Every nerve in my body and every piece of my DNA programmed to breed was screaming at me to take her. I could smell her arousal. It would be so easy to lay her down, fuck her into the ground, and make her cry out my name in ecstasy.

No.

She was obviously having a reaction to the poison, and to take her when she wasn't in her right mind would be incredibly wrong. I wouldn't do that to her or anyone. Grabbing her hands in one of mine, I simply couldn't stand her touching me anymore, my breathing ragged as I struggled to maintain control and keep her still.

I *needed* her to be *still.*

"Ooh yes," she murmured as I closed a fist around her hands. She ground harder into my lap. "Pin my hands while you fuck me. Spank me, nip at my neck, maybe I'll let you fuck my as—"

I slammed my palm over her mouth. "Please," I begged, pushing the words through gritted teeth.

"Stop. Talking."

She continued to grind against me, drawing heavy growls from my chest as my body fought my mind, chest heaving and sweat glistening on my back. I pulled Tori from my lap, stood and looked around wildly for *anything* to restrain her. I stumbled into the woodlands, dragging her with me, and finding nothing, I sighed and sat. With Tori still clutched in my hands, I let my vines wander across her body to restrain her.

The problem was the vines had feeling and senses as part of my body, and as they wound around her wrists and legs, binding her still, I could feel the softness of her skin. She was squirming too much for me to get her clothes back on, so I had to settle for binding her still and draping her tunic over her writhing body. With her restrained, I managed to finish preparing the meal, grinding my teeth the entire time, a muscle in my neck ticking with the strain. The meat burned when I was distracted by the sounds she was making—moans and whimpers of delight—and the sight of her writhing on the ground almost broke me. The heat was heavy in her eyes, and she never stopped looking at me, her pupils still dilated as she stared.

Stripping some of the meat from the carcass, I held it in front of her mouth, begging her to eat.

She did.

Tori took the meat into her mouth, along with my

fingers, swirling her tongue around them and sucking lightly. With a groan, I yanked my hand from her as though burned and waited until she finished the meat before offering her more. Not once did she take her eyes from mine. She moaned, licking her lips obscenely after every mouthful.

When she lost interest in the food and seemed intent only on licking the juices from my fingers, I growled again and finished the meat before putting out the fire.

I held the water bag to her lips. "Drink."

"Nooo," she whined, turning her face away and pouting. "I don't want to."

"You have to drink, Tori. You aren't well."

Her eyes found mine. "But I feel so good." She drew the words out around her tongue, practically purring them out. "Do you know what would make me feel even better?"

I didn't want to hear her talk dirty things anymore, and with a groan, I squeezed the water bag, releasing a rush of the cool liquid into her mouth. Tori coughed and spluttered but swallowed some and then consented to drink a bit more.

"Sleep now," I whispered, my voice gravelly with the effort of containing my desires. Every nerve in my body was on fire, and I couldn't control allowing my vines to stroke against her skin even as I restrained her. Not touching her wasn't an option, and despite the fact I was losing control of my will,

I allowed myself this pleasure.

She continued to squirm, and I kept my hand over her mouth to stop her words, but it didn't stop the moaning sounds she continued to make. It felt like days before she finally slept, and I sunk down next to her, my cock so hard it was aching, drawing my attention to the organ.

Frustration made sleep difficult, and I tightened the grip of my vines around Tori as she slept before I too eventually dozed off.

"Vitri!"

Tori's voice penetrated my consciousness. She sounded panicked, and I sat up abruptly. The sun was peeking over the horizon, casting long shadows through the woodlands. Was there danger? Was she hurt?

"Vitri," Tori cried again. She struggled against the vines, her eyes wide and panicked, although I was thankful her pupils were back to normal. "Why am I tied up? Please, let me go. Please."

I loosened the vines but didn't release them. "How do you feel?"

"How do I feel? Fucking tied up and uncomfortable. Let me go."

Slowly, I released her, the vines sliding back into place around my torso and arms. I watched her cautiously as she pushed herself to her feet, wobbling slightly before righting herself. Tori clutched her head, still glaring at me as though this was my fault and accepted the water bag as I offered it to her, taking a tentative sip.

"Why was I restrained? What happened last night?" She looked at the remnants of the fire and the fur from the gorae. "Why am I *naked?* I don't remember eating, going to bed, or anything."

"You were poisoned."

"By that little plant? But it didn't kill me like you thought it would. I was immune."

I shook my head, my shoulders trembling with the effort to keep calm with the memories of Tori grinding on top of my lap. "It drugged you. You threw yourself at me."

She clasped her hands over her mouth. "Oh my God, did we..."

I snarled as I stood, and she stepped back, eyes wide. "I would *never* take advantage of you." Tori glanced down then, more aware of her nudity than before, and attempted to cover her body with her hands. I wished it were my hands on her.

I snapped.

With a roar, I grabbed her shoulders and walked her backward until her back slammed against a tree on the edge of the woodlands. "Do you have *any* idea how hard it was to resist you?" I leaned in close, deeply inhaling the scent of her hair and skin at the nape of her neck, making her tremble. "You were *begging* me to fuck you. *Begging.*" I released another snarl, and Tori made a slight squeaking sound.

I think I was frightening her, but my control was hanging on by the smallest thread.

And I could smell her arousal.

"I'm sorry," she whispered, trembling. "I didn't do it on purpose."

I grabbed her hands and lifted them above her head, pinning them against the tree. She never took her eyes from mine. There was no fear in them, only determination and heat. "Can you?" I breathed the words out, hovering my hand over her chest, ready to cup her breast.

"Can I what?" Her voice shuddered as my lips came so close to hers.

"Can you do it on purpose? Beg me?" I took another deep inhale of her scent before I licked along the base of her neck and up to her ear. "I need you."

"Vitri..."

"Do you not want me? Do I disgust you?"

"No, no... I *do* want you, it's just..."

We stared at each other for a beat longer, but I never found out what the end of her sentence was. Tori closed the gap between our lips and snaked her tongue into my mouth, forcing my lips apart and deepening the kiss. I groaned against her lips, and with a mammoth effort, pulled away, shaking. "Are you sure you want this?" My grip on her wrists tightened, still held above her head as I took in her body. Her nipples were pointed from arousal, and she was rubbing her thighs together. From the moment I had first seen her, she had awakened something in me I had long forgotten how to feel. Beyond the need to protect and care for her, I needed to *claim* her. Last night, she had almost driven me to the edge, forcing me to fight against the urges built into my DNA and my very being. If I started to take her, I didn't know if I'd be able to stop.

I wouldn't be able to stop.

She had to be sure.

"Are you sure?" I asked again, pulling away a bit and studying her face. "I need you to be sure, or we'll stop right now." I wasn't sure I could, but for her, I would run to the other side of the island if I had to, to keep her safe from me.

She took a shuddering breath, a world of thoughts playing across her face. "I'm sure," she whispered, and her next words broke whatever control I had left. "Please fuck me."

CHAPTER 15

TORI

He became an animal, a constant growl emanating from his large chest as Vitri crushed me against the tree. In the back of my mind, I was vaguely aware we should be walking and keep going on our way toward the ocean to find one of the other girls, but his hand that wasn't pinning mine above my head was exploring my body as his tongue claimed my mouth. When Vitri's large hand encompassed my breast, we moaned, and he brought his fingers together to pinch and twist at my nipple, causing me to cry out. I had no idea what happened last night or what I did that got him so riled up. I kind of wished I remembered so I could do it again because the way he was taking control was ecstasy. There was a hint of roughness to his touch, as though he was aware of how easily he could hurt me but was barely containing himself. It made me feel desirable and powerful, even as I stood trapped between him and a tree, my hands twisting and flexing against his hold in desperation to touch him back.

Vitri moved his hand down, cupping between my legs and casting a glance at me, checking consent or waiting for me to protest. His pupils were wide, taking up almost all of his iris and making him look more monster than man. I only nodded as he snarled again and pressed a large finger inside me. My legs trembled as he pumped his finger in and out, and I'm sure I would've slumped to the ground if he weren't holding me up.

"Vitri," I panted out, squirming against his hold. "Please…"

He grumbled again, no hint of the smirk that usually adorned his face as he watched me come undone under his touch. "You said the other night you would beg me," he whispered, the heat from his breath against my neck making me shudder as he followed it with a lick. "I want to hear you beg."

Oh great, so not only did I land a cheeky-as-fuck alien but a kinky one too.

I pressed my lips together, the expression lasting

only a second as he pressed his finger in deeper, causing me to lift a leg and drape my thigh around his. "Please," I pushed out the word, the humiliation of needing him so bad I was practically keening, coupled with the pleasure of his hand was too much to bear. "Please, Vitri, I need you to fuck me. I need it so bad."

He roared and pulled his hand from mine, grabbed me by the hips, and lifted me, spinning quickly and causing me to yelp as he dropped to his knees and placed me on the ground in front of him. Before I could utter a word, he had spread my thighs with his hands and dived between my legs, licking obscenely at my dripping pussy with long, deliberate licks up and down between my lips. I grabbed onto his braids. "My clit, Vitri, please..."

He lifted himself long enough for me to indicate where I wanted him to touch me before returning his attention to the right spot, pressing and flicking his tongue over my clit, stopping only when he wanted to thrust his tongue inside me. The curl of it played against my G-spot, and I cried out, the growl in his chest increasing in volume.

I wasn't going to last long, and I didn't care. Gripping his braids, I ground my pussy against his face as he returned to my clit. "Fuck, Vitri. Please don't stop!"

Like a punch in the gut, my orgasm hit, making me scream his name as I came hard against his mouth. I was still panting when he crawled over me, his eyes wild, his monstrous cock hard and throbbing, clear precum dripping from the tip. I was ready to beg him again when, with another snarl, he grabbed my hip and flipped me over onto my stomach. I shifted onto my knees, bending over before him and presenting myself to him.

"Take me," I begged, and he responded only with another growl.

The head of his cock pressed against my entrance, and I cried out when he pushed in. He paused for a moment as I took in large lungfuls of air, trying to prepare myself for the stretch. His fingers were big enough, and the head of his cock was huge. But I was dripping wet and ready for him, and after a beat, I pushed back slightly onto him, taking more of him inside me.

Vitri's hands gripped my hips, and with a lurch, he pulled me backward onto his cock until my hips were flush with his. I screamed his name as he penetrated me with a single thrust, my pussy twitching and throbbing around the intrusion. As he began to pull out and thrust slowly, the discomfort eased and was replaced with mind-bending pleasure. His cock wasn't smooth like his skin but ridged, and every drag of him inside me rubbed perfectly against my G-spot. My fingers clenched the yellow grass between them, ripping up the roots and collecting soil under my nails, shuddering and twitching as Vitri fucked me, slowly increasing his speed.

With his hands still on my hips, I felt something brush against my clit and jumped. Looking back, my eyes widened as I saw his vines unwinding from his arms and torso and wrapping around my body, snaking underneath me to brush at my clit while he fucked me.

Holy shit. That should not turn me on as much as it did.

"Vitri, oh my God!" I panted as his vines rubbed against the bundle of nerves.

"Your cunt is so tight," he groaned, pushing in with a particularly hard thrust and holding me in place, forcing me to take it.

When another sensation was added, I turned my head again, panicked. "What are you doing?"

His vines were all around my body now, wrapping around my torso and flicking at my nipples and the underside of my breasts, underneath me and rubbing at my clit, and two were moving across my ass and seeking entrance.

He smirked, but it wasn't the playful smirk I was used to. There was a darkness to his expression and heat in his eyes as he gazed at me, not slowing his thrusts as I squeaked and moaned with every stretch of him. "Last night, you were about to offer me to fuck your ass."

"I did? Oh hell, Vitri, you're too big, I don't think I could…"

He shushed me gently, his fingers tracing across my hips. The slightly bulbous head of one of his vines pressed against my rear entrance, and I gasped when it penetrated. My legs began to tremble with the sensory overload. Vitri was everywhere, all around me, and when two final vines snaked up my body and moved into my mouth, I moaned. They tasted like him, like the delicious scent of him that floated around us as he fucked me harder, musky and sweet.

Vitri had begun to shudder as he thrust into me, groaning and growling like an angry wolf. I went to touch myself as I neared my peak, and vines snatched my hands as I was warned with another growl from Vitri. He held me, his hands on my hips and vines holding my wrists and legs still, the one pumping inside my ass increasing in speed to match his thrusts, and one curling around and flicking at my clit, sending me over the edge.

I came around him, shaking and trembling through my high, panting and crying out his name as the sensations didn't stop but continued to push me past my resistance and send me higher over the edge. With a rumble and a groan, Vitri tilted my hips up, his final thrusts becoming sporadic before he came inside me, the volume of his cum forcing it out around his cock and leaking down my legs.

As his vines retreated from my body and he pulled out, I collapsed onto my stomach, my legs twitching intermittently as aftershocks of pleasure pulsed through my worn body.

Vitri lay over me, his wet cock rubbing between my ass cheeks as he kissed my neck. I hummed appreciatively of his gentle caresses and the feel of his velvety smooth skin against my back as he quietly chuckled.

"Ready to walk?" he said, laughing again when I groaned and buried my face in the crook of my elbow. I wasn't sure my legs would even work properly, let alone allow me to walk for a few days. "Or if you like..." he pushed against me, my hips pressing into the grass as I felt every line of his cock between my cheeks. "We could go again."

"I think you'll have to carry me," I mumbled against my arm, my eyes closed and feeling like I could drift off into a peaceful, exhausted sleep right now. I groaned again when he lifted his weight from me, the rush of cool air against the sweat on my back making me shiver. He came around in front of me, helping me to my feet with one hand and offering me my clothes with the other. I didn't want it to be over. I ached with the loss of him inside me, and the way he held my gaze told me he felt the same. I knew we couldn't stay here fucking all day, but I'd be lying if I said I didn't want to.

We stood chest to chest, and I could feel the

increased beating of his heart against me. I took a moment to revel in the feel of him against me and traced my fingers up his arm, eliciting another delicious growl from him. His vines were back in place, wrapped around his arms, and I danced my fingers across them. With a look that was both sad and frustrated, Vitri took a half step away from me, and when I whimpered, he smiled that dark grin again.

I'd have him again soon.

I nodded as he indicated to my shoes and put them on before taking a long gulp from the water bag. It was time to go. We had important things to do, and although my clit throbbed and my pussy ached so fucking good, I had to remember why we were taking this journey. When I began to walk, I held my hand up, stopping him in his tracks as he followed. "Just give me a minute," I said, stepping behind a bush for a moment of privacy, although my legs still shook, and I needed to lean against the tree.

When I came back, Vitri immediately pulled me against him, running his fingers through my short hair and pressing his tongue into my mouth. He tasted like me, and I moaned against him.

"Let's get going, Tori. We have to make up time." He growled as he pressed his lips to my neck, dragging his teeth along my collarbone. "If we make it halfway through these woodlands before sundown, I'll reward you tonight."

I hummed, my eyes fluttering closed for a moment before he took my hand, and we began to walk.

I'll give him this—Vitri sure knew how to offer motivation.

CHAPTER 16

VITRI

Tori continued to push herself past what I expected of her as we walked. I slowed my pace to allow her to keep up, but she still pushed harder even when the terrain became as uneven as her breathing. Tori only accepted taking a break when I insisted on it and claimed that I also needed to rest, although I think she knew I was lying. I sat on the ground cross-legged and pulled her onto my lap, her back pressed against my chest. Tori laughed and squirmed for a moment before settling against me as I wrapped my arms around her, pulling her closer still and breathing in her delicious scent.

She wanted to find her other friends, and I wanted to help her, but my mind had become foggy since we fucked, and the feel of her body against mine was all I could think about now. Ilk was always more levelheaded than me, and now that I was in the presence of a gorgeous female whose attraction to me was excelled only by my reaction to her, I was reverting to what I was created to be. The scent of my pheromones drifted from my skin, every pore saturated the air and tried to lure Tori to me again, my body acting on my subconscious desires, even as I attempted to remain strong. All I wanted to do was fuck her again and again and again until she couldn't take any more pleasure and her belly was rounded with child.

My child.

Before we came to rest, every step as we walked was agony for me. Maybe it wasn't a complete lie that I also needed a break. However, I didn't need a break from the journey, I needed a break from the constant screaming of my mind to take Tori again. I had moved behind her as we walked so I could keep an eye on her and catch her if she tripped on the uneven ground. But it also meant I had spent hours watching the shape of her ass and legs moving in front of me, muscles twisting and flexing as she ambled over the ground as it shifted between rocky crevices around woody tree trunks and short, uncomfortable bushes that scraped her skin. But she never complained, and I bit back a moan when I thought I should've been smart enough to make her a pair of pants like Erica's instead of a tunic. Selfishly, I had thought I could keep her with me in my home, and although I understood her desire to seek out her friends, I only wanted to keep her with me.

Keeping Tori safe from the Ghaal was my priority, and while a rebellious part of me felt my home was high and secluded enough to keep her safe, Ilk was right—we had to keep moving, at least for now.

"Vitri, we need to get something to eat," Tori whined, squirming hard after a brief rest to get out of my grasp and off my lap. It only made me hold her tighter, pulling her body flush against mine as a small growl rumbled through my throat.

"There's only one thing I want to eat," I grumbled out and growled long and low at how she laughed and rolled her shoulder up to her neck when I nibbled at the sensitive skin under her ear.

"I'm serious." She finally pushed herself from my grasp, standing abruptly and turning to face me with her hands on her hips. "Is there something around here we can eat? Then we can get going again." The tilt of her hips had me mesmerized, and I was no longer watching her face, only the image of her delicate fingers on her hip, exactly where I had held her earlier as I fucked her sweet cunt.

"Vitri?"

I tried to shake the thoughts from my head because she wanted an answer. Tori was talking to me.

Think. Focus.

I needed to feed and look after her. How was she to bear my child when she had no strength? She needed to eat.

Tori bent over so we were face to face, her eyes widening as a snarl I couldn't control escaped my lips. When she bent like that, I could see her breasts as the tunic fell forward.

"Are you okay?" she whispered and touched my face.

Please don't touch me. I might just lose control.

My Tori was talking to me. I should respond, but my shoulders shook as I battled to keep myself under control. Did I need to repeat to myself that I am an intelligent being, like some sort of mantra to keep me in line? I'm smarter than this. I can control this. *I can.* I may have been created for breeding, but my intelligence outweighs that of my creators.

I adapt, I learn, I integrate. I am the best genetic engineering has to offer.

And above all, I am here to protect Tori.

Even if that includes protecting her from me.

Did I really lose myself so much during the time I was separated from my brothers? We split up in order to cover more of the island and protect those abducted from other planets. But were my brothers aware of something I was not? I knew we could change genders if required, so if left alone in a group, half of us would likely change, and we would pair up and breed with each other, especially now after time apart. What if we got together and our bodies and instincts took over, and it became nothing more than a mad mating frenzy? Not ideal when we were trying to keep our minds clear to stop innocents from falling victim to the Ghaal.

Ilk didn't seem this crazy with Erica. How had he done it? Why hadn't I thought to ask?

I clenched my teeth. But I was thinking clearly enough to know I *should've* asked Ilk. That was something, and it was something I could cling to while I watched Tori in front of me, her expression unclear in the haze of my mind, although I'm sure it would be one of concern.

It was like my personality had come rushing back to me the day I began following Tori after she landed. Little pieces of me falling into place to create the whole and complete being that I am—the Synth I forgot I was—the instinct, the intelligence, and the personality.

But once Tori let me inside her, there was another change.

And now, every breath was a constant battle for control not to take her again. I would never hurt her, not ever. But the pull of her body was strong, and the reminder of her taste every time I picked up a hint of her scent in the wind was enough to make my knees buckle.

I still hadn't responded to her, and she kept saying my name. I could hear it through the fog in my mind, her voice fading in and out. My name sounded so sweet coming from her. I never thought much of names, but now I loved my name and craved hearing it from her lips.

Tori kneeled in front of me, and when I simply continued to stare at her, eyes blazing with lust, she cupped my cheeks in her hands. I should stop her from touching me, but the warmth that flared under her palm had me groaning.

"Vitri," she repeated my name again from those lips, lips I wanted to touch, to kiss, to feel wrapped around my cock. I raised my hands to mirror her hold on me and brushed my thumb over her lips, pressing against the soft flesh. The concern never left her eyes. Wasn't she wonderful? Still caring about me. "Are you okay? Please talk to me."

Now her tone was edged in panic, and I wanted to soothe her because that's what a good mate should do—look after, feed, and find shelter for his mate, but also take care of her, make sure she is calm and happy, and at her most content at all times. I tried to form words, but instead, my tongue flickered obscenely with the memory of doing the same motion against her sweet cunt, and her cheeks flushed.

Gently, I pulled Tori's face to mine and planted a tender kiss on her lips. She returned it with little enthusiasm, still staring at me with intense compassion and concern. Still holding her face, I ran my tongue over her lips, and this made her shudder and her eyes flutter closed for a moment. An almost inaudible growl vibrated through my chest, and I repeated the action, sliding my tongue past her lips when she gasped. With a hand behind her head, I thrust my tongue into her mouth, causing her to squeak and her eyes widen as I kissed her hard.

I kept going, and she moaned against my lips, the sound so sweet that another tremble passed down my spine. With one hand, I pawed at her breasts, fighting the fabric to move out of the way so I could have the skin-on-skin contact I so desperately needed. In the back of my mind, there was a battle raging. If I took Tori again now, would my control over myself be better or worse? Would I descend further into the breeding machine I was created to be with every touch of her? Or could I fuck it out of my system? How long would it take? A day? A night? A full cycle of the moon?

We pulled away from each other at the same time, and her eyes wildly searched mine for answers since I still hadn't said anything. With a hard shove, Tori pushed my shoulders. "Talk to me!"

I needed control.

With a mammoth effort, I pulled myself to my feet. Tori stepped back and looked up as I drew myself to my full height, towering over her. Kneeling on the ground like that, she was the perfect height for me to slide my cock into her waiting mouth. I wondered what the warmth and wetness of her mouth around me would feel like.

No.

When I snatched my spear up, she glanced at me wearily, but I was thankful to note she didn't flinch or move away.

She knew I wouldn't hurt her.

The thought sent another surge of animalistic possessiveness through me, and with a roar, I lifted my spear, bringing it down and slicing deep through my calf muscle. As I collapsed to my knees, drinking in the agony as my blood spilled down my leg, the stinging shock of the pain brought reality crashing back. Tori shrieked and launched herself at me. With one hand, I was able to hold her at arm's length, and she continued to fight against me, reaching out and desperate to tend to my self-inflicted wound.

I drank in the moment. I lived in the pain, breathed sharply through my teeth, and ignored the feel of her body pushed against my palm, her arms reaching out.

Ignore how she reaches for you, how she cares.

Focus on the pain. It burns.

Good, let it burn some more.

"Tori." She stilled as I finally spoke, my voice gravelly. "I'm sorry."

The fog from my mind cleared somewhat, enough for me to think straight for the moment, and as I let Tori go, she stumbled slightly and regained her footing. Her eyes were a mixture of anger, confusion, and pain, and I grimaced, hating myself for being the cause of that for her as I tore a thin strip from my loin cloth and wrapped it around the wound. Tying it tight, I managed to stem the flow of blood and snarled when another shot of pain fired through my muscles as I finished the knot. But it was a good, distracting pain, and I breathed in harshly through clenched teeth and focused on it, gaining more control with each breath.

I stood and dropped my arms so Tori could approach me, which she did in a rush, slamming her palms against my chest and crying out, "What the fuck was that? Were you in some sort of trance? *Tell me.*" Her palms were wandering over my chest, and I was able to keep control.

Focus on the throbbing of the wound. Breathe in. Breathe out.

"Tell me *now* because if it happens again, I need to know what to do!" she cried out.

Dipping my chin to my chest, I took another moment to collect myself. She had every right to be angry. There was so much about this planet she didn't know, so much about *me*. What she had learned in these past days was barely scratching the surface. How could you ever learn everything about a planet anyway? A being without enhanced learning abilities had no chance, especially not for a planet littered with an eclectic mixture of species from all the galaxies. I was her stability, and I had vowed to look after her.

Yet I had lost control, and she had lost the one thing she could rely on.

Me.

"I'm sorry," I repeated, and I meant it with every fiber of my being. How could I explain to her what had happened without her worrying it would happen again?

How did I know it wouldn't?

"I was created for breeding," I said, and Tori nodded, her palms still pressed against my chest, the warmth both a comfort and a curse.

"You told me that already."

"Please. Listen." I was still gaining back my control, focusing on every throb of pain that ebbed from my wound to keep me in line. Had Ilk had this problem too? Somehow, I doubted it. We were created from a mixture of Ghaal and synthetic DNA, and each of us was as different from each other as any other beings. Ilk always had more control, was more levelheaded, the leader, and stronger. I again cursed myself for not asking him how to keep control while I had the chance, but I never thought I would lose it so quickly.

I never thought Tori would feel so good stretched around my cock.

Concentrate!

"I was created for breeding," I repeated, trying to keep my thoughts clear. "Our personalities were an accident almost, a side effect of our synthetic DNA and intelligence. I've been alone so long, the part of me that runs purely on instinct had been pushed to the side, almost forgotten. Until you." I paused, looking at Tori, still watching me with eyes full of concern. I slammed down a mental block to stop the flood of inappropriate thoughts from taking over. "You... reactivated me in a way. I'm responding to you the way I was designed to respond to females. Then when you let me inside you..." I growled, low and deep, lifting a lip in a snarl that sent a shudder down her spine. But she didn't break eye contact or move away. "It was cemented, and now, it's all I can think about. Taking over my thoughts until I'm barely more than an animal. I'm sorry I scared you..." I indicated my bandaged leg, "... but I needed to regain control, to distract myself, and it was all I could think of in the moment."

Tori shook her head. "I don't understand. Why

me? There have been other females kidnapped and dropped here from your own admission. So why didn't they do this to you? Why aren't you off fucking those banshees who attacked me and stole my robe?"

I ran my hands over my face. "Because unlike them and every other species that's been abandoned here, you are compatible with the Ghaals for breeding." *And therefore, compatible with me too.* I didn't voice it. Was that to protect her or me from the truth? Was I worried she wouldn't want me again? How could I even be sure she was compatible just because we fit together?

I knew.

I just knew.

I felt it within me.

"Which the Ghaal know too," Tori said, interrupting my once again drifting thoughts.

"Yes."

"All the more reason we need to eat and *get the fuck going,* Vitri! Find the others."

"I know, I know," I snarled, already battling anger and guilt and not needing Tori's reminder of how I am failing as a mate to her—not providing enough, not caring for enough.

I wasn't enough.

She wrapped her arms around my middle and squeezed, and for a moment, I was caught off guard by the gesture, and there was a pause before I returned the hug. Without pulling away, she asked, "So if you lose control again, I don't have to stab you, do I?"

"Because you'd hate that so much."

She chuckled before sighing. "I would, actually."

I pulled away from her, grabbed her hand, and led her off in search of food. "If it happens again, and you can't snap me out of it, then yes, stab me as hard as you can. I promise I can take it."

Her expression suggested she hoped I was joking before her eyes widened with realization.

What I didn't want to tell her was the fears nagging in my mind.

What if I was flawed? Unlike the other Synths and unable to keep my instincts under control with intelligence?

What if what I should have said to Tori was, if she was unable to get me under control, to *run?*

What if the second biggest threat to her on this planet was me?

CHAPTER 17

TORI

Vitri hunted, and he let me trail along but didn't allow me to take the kill. My aim with the spear was still pretty far off, and I wasn't even sure I could throw it with enough strength to make a clean kill. He found a group of ground dwellers like the creature I had killed when I first came here and took two of them to cook for us. We ate in silence, and I thanked Vitri with every strip of meat he handed me, clean and cooked to perfection, although bland without the spices and seasonings I would've added back on Earth. But he said nothing in response, lost in his thoughts once again. At least this time, his eyes didn't have that glazed look as though he were a million miles away.

I trusted Vitri to keep himself under control, although the ache between my legs made thoughts whisper in my mind about how it wouldn't be *such* a bad thing to let him lose a bit of control with me. If the way he had fucked me earlier had been him *with* control, I could only dream of what he would be like if he let that thread of control slip just a little bit—enough for me to get a peek of the animal underneath, the part of him that ran only on instinct.

Kicking dirt over the remnants of the fire, I took a grateful swig from my water bag, trying not to let concern flood me at how empty I felt before we began walking again. Vitri's arm twitched with every few steps as though he wanted to hold my hand or place his palm on my lower back but didn't trust himself to. Just as often, I was tempted to instigate the contact, but then I would remember his roar as he stabbed himself with his spear and his blood running down his leg while he drank in the pain to bring himself under control.

I didn't want to be the reason he had to do that again.

We walked, encountering several species along the way, many of which were mostly harmless unless engaged, or so Vitri said. I trusted him enough, keeping my distance from the species to avoid accidentally gaining more attention than I was after.

When we finally came to a stream, water trickling down between the mossy rocks and shrubs, I felt a renewed surge of energy. I'd finished my water, and although I knew Vitri would let me have some of his, it was difficult not to feel like I was already too much of a burden on him without taking his water too. The man—or alien, whatever—had left his home to help me search for my friends. Girls I admittedly didn't really know but were the closest things to friends or family I had here. I needed to know they were safe. It wouldn't be enough for me to live out here with Vitri or Erica and Ilk, not knowing if Samara and Misha were safe. We could decide what we wanted to do next once we were all together. Although we apparently needed to keep moving for a while, never settling in one place too long, like an extended camping trip, I guess. I understood the idea behind the plan, but it concerned me too. What if our constantly moving about only made the Ghaal more desperate? What if they resorted to some really messed-up measures to get us?

Vitri and I still hadn't spoken much since his episode earlier today. He'd been informative when I'd asked him questions about plants or wildlife, but his voice remained deadpan as though he was reading from a script.

He was trying not to engage with me too much, and although I now understood the reasons, I can't say it didn't hurt. Not after we'd had sex.

Kneeling next to the stream, I held my water bag under the steady trickle as it flowed over a series of rocks and filled it partially, taking a huge mouthful and gulping it down loudly before filling the bag again. I caught Vitri's gaze out of the corner of my eye, and for a moment, I'm certain he had that smirk I had grown to love plastered on his face. But it disappeared as quickly as it had come, and instead, he offered me a small half-smile, which simply wasn't the same.

I didn't want him to recede into himself because he was afraid, but I didn't know what to do to make it right. Evidently, my sheer presence here was a test to him, and only he could figure out how to control instincts he'd been able to ignore for so long.

Who would've thought my biggest concern on an alien planet would be not to hurt a sexy alien man's feelings?

Water bag full, I stood and brushed the leaves and moss from my knees. I desperately wanted to rest, but I knew if I stopped again today, I wouldn't want to go again until after some sleep. Glancing up, I couldn't see the sun's position in the sky, and the light that dappled through the woodlands cast long shadows on the trees. Not much longer now until we could rest, I guessed.

"We'll stop for the night soon, Tori." Vitri's soothing voice came as if reading my thoughts while he stood behind me, brushing his fingertips down my arm. I shuddered, and his hand jumped from me as though he had been shocked. He muttered something in a language I didn't understand and took a step back, his absence from me obvious as the cool breeze whipped against my back.

Dammit, I wanted him to stay close.

What were these bullshit feelings?

Looking up when I heard music, I scanned the area, unable to see anything unusual. "Vitri..." He glanced at me, coming a step closer, and I reached out, grabbing his arm. "Where is that music coming from?"

"The asha."

It was entrancing—soft voices and light whistles intertwined to create a song that called to me and could lull me to sleep if I let it. Every muscle in my body calmed while Vitri seemed to tense further. "Are they dangerous? Can we see them?"

I had no idea exactly what *they* were, but something about the song made me long to see where it emanated from, even to touch or embrace them if I could. Vitri growled, low and quiet, a barely-there sound. "They are quite beautiful. I will take you to see them if you promise to stay by my side."

I should be moving on with our journey, getting as close as we could before nightfall. But I simply *had* to see the asha. I had to. I wouldn't be able to rest, eat, or sleep until I did. It struck me for just a moment the desire to see them should concern me like they were somehow drugging me with their voices. But then the music would drift between the trees again, and all I wanted to do was find the source. Vitri took my hand then and held it tightly in his as he walked me upstream. It was the first real physical contact we'd had in hours, but his shoulders and arms were still tense.

"They sing because they smell my pheromones," he explained, pulling me along behind him, but stepping carefully, I tried to mimic his strides. "Once they see it's me, a Synth, they will stop. They know we are not compatible as mates."

"Are they another kidnapped species?"

"Yes, four of them live here, each as beautiful as the last. I can see why the Moeks were drawn to them."

Something that resembled jealousy bristled inside me at Vitri referring to the asha as *beautiful,* but I refused to be jealous over my alien man.

Shit, there it was again.

My alien man.

Fuck, I was in deep.

"Do the Moeks just kidnap species willy-nilly?"

Vitri frowned at me, and I wished he would grin again—that smirk that made his eyes sparkle with mischief. In trying to keep himself under control, he had become so serious, a wall of stone of nothingness, and I longed for the spark of personality from him that made me feel alive. "Willy-nilly?"

"Randomly. Like, do they just go planet hopping, taking random females of random species, hoping one of them will match?"

He shook his head. "There is a particular method to it, certain shared DNA sequences that they would be looking for or physical traits. We left the Ghaal colony before they began searching, so I don't know their exact selection criteria."

"What about the giant beetle thing that exploded into jelly?"

"The lupher?" He chuckled, that grin settling onto his face for longer than it had in hours before he again brought himself into line. "I have no idea. Desperation? Maybe the Moeks had a duty to bring back *something,* and when they couldn't find anything suitable, they just grabbed whatever they could."

"Willy-nilly," I said, grinning.

He returned the smile, and I held his eye contact for as long as he would let me. "Willy-nilly."

We stopped as the rush from the stream grew

more insistent, barreling over larger rocks. The singing was still coming, louder now, but still somehow playing in the background of my awareness, as though part of a dream. "Don't get too close. They'll attempt to seduce you regardless of your gender or species."

"Vitri, I'm hardly going to fu—"

He slapped a hand over my mouth, and I was too late to stifle my moan at the move. His pupils dilated, and he snarled before closing his eyes and taking a few deep breaths. When he opened his eyes, his pupils were back to normal, but his gaze was still drenched with desire. "I'm going to have to ask you not to say that word around me, Tori." His voice was heavy with lust, and I trembled under his gaze and the dark intentions behind it, nodding and sucking in a breath when he pulled his hand away.

With a nod, we came out from behind the trees, and I gasped again.

Vitri was right—the asha were beautiful.

Like Vitri and myself, they were humanoid in appearance—two legs and two arms. The four women sat together in the middle of the stream, that beautiful music coming from their mouths which remained open but otherwise unmoving. Only the twitching muscles in their throat showed any evidence they were creating the music. The one closest eyes fell upon me, and I shuddered. Her eyes were pitch black but glittering as though the stars lived in her gaze. Their skin was greenish but almost pale gray as the light shifted around them when they moved, and as they sang, they ran their fingers through their silky black hair that hung down to their waists. They were naked except for a smattering of jewelry-like garments, strings that wrapped around their waists and upper arms laden with beads, feathers, and fur.

Their faces were sheer perfection of symmetrical beauty that was difficult to pull my gaze from.

Compatible or not, I can understand why the Moeks were drawn to them.

The singing stopped, and the one closest dragged her gaze lazily to Vitri. She purred out his name, and although it sounded strange and ethereal, it was definitely his name. Jealousy blossomed in my chest again, and I tried to remind myself that Vitri had communicated with as many species who landed on this planet as he could. Vitri shook his head at her, and when the asha's gaze returned to me, I grabbed his hand defiantly, making sure she saw. She looked amused for a moment, then turned back to the other asha, and they began to talk to each other, no longer singing. As Vitri had predicted, they were no longer interested in us.

I stared at them for a moment longer. Despite my jealousy at her saying his name, I was still entranced by their beauty before Vitri tugged my hand and pulled me back the way we had come.

"She knew your name," I said, once I thought—hoped—we were out of earshot of the asha.

"Many species do. I try to talk to as many as I can to protect them from the Ghaal." He looked down at me, frowning. "You know all of this." When I was unable to control my expression, he grinned, and I seethed as realization dawned on him. "You were *jealous,*" Vitri teased, poking my arm gently and chuckling. "Tori was jealous of another female talking to me." I scowled at his teasing until his grin dropped, and his gaze fell to our intertwined fingers. "You were jealous over me..." he whispered. A shudder ran up his spine, and he pulled his hand from mine slowly and purposefully.

I wanted to defend myself, to say anything to bring back control when my feelings had been so blatantly on display. But all I could manage was his name before he interrupted me. "Vitri—"

"Come," he said, his tone clipped and grin gone. "We'll cover as much ground as we can before nightfall."

CHAPTER 18

TORI

Vitri's mood deteriorated as the next couple of hours wore on. His limp hadn't lasted long after he had stabbed himself in the leg, and while he must be a fast healer, I was glad he was no longer in pain. I gripped my spear at the memory. He told me I might need to be the one to hurt him, to stab at him and inflict pain as though he were the enemy on this planet.

Nothing Vitri had done had led me to believe I was in danger around him. He had even resisted me when I was apparently coming on to him under the influence of that stupid poison plant last night. But he had said things were different now—something had changed after we had fucked, and now he was struggling to keep control. I could see it in his eyes. Vitri watched me as we walked, rarely side by side, and most of the time he was behind me. Now and then I would turn to look at him, and his gaze would be hungry and predatory. Then he would see me watching and shake his head as if to shake his thoughts loose. But he never got rid of them. The dangerous look in his eyes only increased with every hour that passed.

We stopped for a short break, and when I sat to have a snack and a drink, Vitri took several more purposeful steps past me and sat several feet away with his back to me.

Tutting, I stood and came up behind him. As I lifted a hand to touch his shoulder, he whipped around, snatched my wrist, and stopped me before I touched his velvety skin.

"Vitri," I started, unsure what exactly I was going to say.

"Don't."

Anger bubbled inside me, mingling with rejection. "We can't keep going like this. Let me help you get this under control."

"You can't help." Vitri shoved my hand away, and pain flared in his eyes at the motion at the same time as rage crossed mine.

"You don't know that. You, yourself, said you've never had this reaction with someone else, which, by the way, I find hard to believe. How do you know you can't be helped?"

The pain in his gaze was replaced with anger. "You don't believe it's only *you* I can't control myself around?"

"That's not... Vitri, that's not even what I'm talking about. I can help."

He stood, and I took an immediate step back, all at once intimidated and caught off guard by his height and sheer size. I backtracked as quickly as he approached and closed the gap between us until my back hit a tree, and I yelped. Vitri's hand trembled, twitching as though he wanted to touch me but thought better of it. "You think *any* female would do this to me?"

I was tired of the allegations like this was somehow my fault. "*I'm* not doing anything to you. You're doing this to yourself."

I've never been caught in the intense stare of a lion as it was about to hunt down its prey, but as I stared into Vitri's gaze, I think I had a pretty good idea what it might feel like. His voice had become animalistic, laced with growls and snarls at my perceived challenge of his partnership with me. I held up my hands in a gesture of surrender, but I could see it was already too late to calm him. My fingers curled around the spear I still held, and Vitri caught the movement with his eye.

"Vitri..." I whispered.

Was I no longer safe with him? His breathing was heavy and ragged. Everything had gone downhill in a matter of minutes, and now I was fighting the urge to flee from the danger he presented, the darkness rolling off him in waves.

"Run," he whispered, the words barely a hint against the breeze.

"W-what?" I asked. But he didn't answer, only ducked his head as a series of growls emanated from his barrel-like chest. I lifted my spear with a shaking hand, trying to at least portray the threat I would attack him if I needed to, although every nerve in my body was screaming at me not to hurt him.

I didn't fight the urge a second time.

I ran.

Vitri wasn't far behind me. I could hear him crashing through the trees, showing none of the care he did the first time I had seen him move. In his forest, he had swayed and swerved carefully around every plant as though they were a part of him, and I suppose they were. That forest was his home. But now he was an animal coming after its prey.

Me.

What would happen if he caught me? He wouldn't hurt me—he said he would look after me. He *promised.* But a promise means nothing when all control is lost, and instinct has taken over. An instinct that has been programmed in him and was taking over his being.

I was sure he wouldn't hurt me.

At least not on purpose.

I was as sure as I could be while fleeing through a strange woodland with an alien twice my size chasing me.

But he might hurt me accidentally. He was huge and intent on fucking me. What if he couldn't hold back? What if he tore me apart in a fit of passion?

I ran, but my lungs were already beginning to burn, and I couldn't keep this up for long.

Vitri wanted me to stab him, and I might not be left with a choice.

Clutching my spear, I pushed myself and continued running for as long as I could, but I was putting off the inevitable, and Vitri didn't seem like he was going to gain control of himself any time soon. Every now and then, the growls from him would be punctuated by a frustrated roar, and his steps would falter and stumble. He was trying *so hard* not to pursue me, but he couldn't help it. He'd asked me to take action if he ever got out of control, and I owed him this.

Before I could overthink it too much more, I stopped and spun on the spot, crouching low and holding the spear out, ready. *In the leg,* I repeated to myself, I didn't want to kill him, *just stab him in the leg. Hard. He said he could take it.*

He promised.

Only seconds passed before Vitri came into view, and his wild gaze scanned the area, seeing me a moment too late as I lunged forward and drove the head of my spear into his calf. He cried out, and I pressed my hands over my ears, biting back the need to sob at the sounds of his pained cries and knowing it was me who caused him that pain. I didn't want to hurt him, but I had to.

I was *forced* to.

No matter how much I told myself I had no other choice, the sound of his primal wailing as he stumbled away was imprinted in my mind, and I sunk near the base of the nearest tree and cried.

Was nowhere on this planet safe?

CHAPTER 19

VITRI

Abruptly and with a massive dose of pain to keep me in check, clarity returned.

Stumbling to my feet, I reached down and removed Tori's spear from my calf, snarling as I did so, the pointed edge catching on the muscle and bringing a steady flow of blood once removed. Undoing the bandage I had on my other leg, I used the same scrap of material to cover the newly bleeding wound, intentionally tying it tight and yanking, inflicting myself with another sharp dose of pain.

Twice so soon I had lost control.

Turning, I sniffed the air. The winds were rising, preparing for the nightly onslaught of extreme weather. Tori must've been downwind from me, and I couldn't smell her. "Tori?" I called out. There was no direct answer but a muted shuffling sound, small feet dragging through the undergrowth. Moving toward the sound, I pushed the thin trees out of my way, needing to get back to her now that my head was clear. "Tori?"

"I'm…" her voice trailed off, and I could almost picture her biting her bottom lip in indecision. She was hesitant to reveal her location to me, and the revelation filled me with self-loathing. When she spoke up again, her voice was stronger, more assured.

She had decided to keep trusting me.

"I'm here," she cried out, shuffling increasing as she moved to meet me halfway.

When she came into my sight, I groaned, and Tori stopped dead at the sound, one hand braced on a tree trunk and her knees bent slightly as though preparing to flee again. I held my hands up between us in surrender as I had seen her do before.

"I'm sorry. I'm sorry. The sound was just a reaction to seeing you hurt."

"I'm not hurt." Her lie was revealed as she took another step and flinched when the many grazes and cuts on her legs dragged across yet another harsh bush. "It's nothing." With apparent effort, she wiped her expression clear, concern returning when she looked at my leg. "Are you okay? I didn't hurt you too badly, did I?"

When we reached each other, I handed Tori's spear to her, and she eyed the end, dark with my blood, before hesitantly accepting the weapon. "You hurt me just enough."

I was a danger to her, but there were other dangers on this island she couldn't protect herself from. Despite a part of the logical part of my mind, the part that hadn't been taken over with my feelings for Tori, telling me to leave, I didn't want to. I simply needed to do better. Tori needed me to protect her, to keep her safe, and I couldn't do that when I couldn't think straight.

Tori's cheeks flared pink as I watched her, and she rubbed an elbow as she tore her gaze from mine, her lips moving with unasked questions.

"Talk to me, Tori."

"It's just..." she trailed off, the color on her cheeks intensifying. "Aw, hell." Tori lifted her head to look at me, her expression flat. "You were getting worse as the day went on, and I can't help but wonder if it wasn't me who made it worse for you."

My brows drew together. "What are you talking about?"

"Maybe it was the asha, their song or something..."

She must've realized how ridiculous her statement was the second the words left her lips, for she looked at the ground again, muttering curses under her breath. Tori really was jealous of them or even the prospect I could be attracted to them. This wasn't about me but her trying to find out how much connection I had with other females.

No matter how many times I told her there were no other females for me, it apparently wasn't enough.

My lip lifted into a silent snarl. I grabbed her upper arm and began marching back the way we'd come. "Come with me."

"Where are we going?"

"Back to the asha so I can prove to you they do nothing for me."

Tori pulled against my grip, and when she tried to stop walking, her heels dragged along in the soil. "No, Vitri, please. You don't have to. I shouldn't have said anything. It was a stupid question." When I ignored her, she struggled anew, attempting to pry my fingers off her arm. "This is a waste of time, Vitri. It's not important."

Spinning to face her, Tori ran into my chest, looking up at me as I wrapped my vines around her, holding her close. "You don't understand, do you? The *only one* who makes me lose control is you. The *only one* I care about keeping safe is *you.* If we have to walk this entire trip a hundred times over for me to prove that to you, I will."

We stared at each other for a long while, Tori's pupils darting back and forth as she studied my face. After a while, her shoulders dropped, and she sagged into my touch, resting her cheek against my chest.

"I believe you," she whispered, tracing small circles around my vines with the fingers on her free hand. "I promise I believe you. We don't need to walk all the way back to the asha. Please, Vitri, let's keep moving forward."

I stared at her and with a nod, I unwrapped her arms from around me, turned her around, and nudged her in the direction we were walking to find her friends. "This way."

CHAPTER 20

VITRI

Pulling Tori to a stop as the last of the light disappeared behind the tree line, she sank gratefully to the ground, removing her shoes and massaging her feet. I had kept her walking longer than I should have, but once again, after the visit to the asha when Tori had shown a streak of jealousy over *me,* I had almost lost control again. So close after regaining the control, the way Tori had been unable to hide her possessiveness over *me* almost pushed me over the edge.

I needed to do better. I owed her that. The

frightened look in Tori's eyes haunted my memories.

I must do better.

"Stay here," I commanded Tori, who threw me a look halfway between defiance and concern before I crashed through the undergrowth to gather some food. There would be no hunting tonight as I don't think I could summon the concentration to do it. Efficiently, I found a selection of foods we could eat raw, returned to where we were making camp for the night, and dropped the bundle on the ground in front of Tori. She lowered her water bag, finishing her mouthful and wiping her lips with the back of her hand before glaring at me. I knew I was throwing my weight around like I was having a tantrum, but the fog was taking over my mind again, and I was rallying my strength to keep myself coherent long enough until we could fall asleep.

I'm sure I would feel better in the morning.

I hoped.

Tori ate. Several times she looked as though she was about to start a conversation and then stopped herself. Guilt now mingled with my existing conflict of emotions. I liked Tori, loved her even, and here I was treating her terribly because I could not control myself.

When we had eaten and Tori had excused herself to step behind a tree for a moment, we settled down to sleep. I lay down, folding my hands behind my head and locking my fingers together, staring at the stars and watching the galaxies in the distance, wondering if one of them contained Tori's home planet and if she missed it. I imagine she did, and again, I should be comforting her, not lying here battling my urges.

Again, I had failed as a mate.

Maybe after we found Tori's friends, I should leave her with them under Ilk's protection. I wasn't good enough for her, not like this.

I kept my gaze trained toward the sky as Tori shuffled around next to me, I assumed trying to find a comfortable spot. I wanted to cuddle into her, and I would have to when the night winds picked up. But I couldn't do it while she was awake and squirming against me, igniting my every nerve on fire with her movements.

"Vitri," she whispered from somewhere next to me.

"What is it, Tori?" I tried my best to keep my voice calm but knew from her hesitation in responding I sounded angry. I hoped she could forgive me when I finally figured out how to control this.

"Vitri, look at me."

Rolling my head to the side, I gasped, a sound which quickly turned into a growl as I scrambled into a crouch and moved away from her. She was naked, standing above me, her skin almost glowing in the light of the moon and the stars. "Tori," I gasped out her name, looking at the ground and curling my fingers around the undergrowth, hoping to ground myself. "What are you doing?"

When I raised my eyes to hers, trying and failing not to let my gaze wander over the curves and lines of her body, her expression was determined, even if her voice was timid. "Would it help..." she swallowed before straightening her posture and starting again, "Would it help keep you under control if we had sex?"

"Tori..." Her name was nothing but a growl from between clenched teeth, and I trembled through the next few seconds, my pheromones tumbling over the air between us and meeting her intoxicating scent halfway.

She stepped forward, and I shuffled away, standing and backing up against a tree, pressing my fingers against the texture of it, desperately trying to focus on anything but her. "Maybe you'll be able to keep better control if you... give in a little, you know? If we have sex a couple of times a day... maybe?" Her voice trailed off into nothing, and when I raised my head to face her again, my expression was dark.

"Run."

"What?"

I straightened, and her eyes followed the movement until I towered over her, twitching with every ounce of strength it was taking me not to attack her right now. "Run, Tori. Run from me. I'll find you in the morning. Run and hide."

Every word was agony to get out, but that pain was nothing compared to the shock of her taking a step toward me. "No." She was trembling, but her expression was still filled with determination. She took another step, then another, and placed a warm palm on my chest, causing another avalanche of growls to shudder through me. "Not this time." Her breathy whisper was destroying what was left of my self-control. "Take me, Vitri."

"Please," I pleaded with her, shaking almost uncontrollably now. "Please leave."

Her voice was husky and filled with lust. "Don't push me away. Why don't you trust yourself?"

My eyes closed. Tori's scent was temporarily wiped from my mind, replaced with the memories of the lab we were created in. The cages, the instruments of torture, the constant reminder from the Ghaal they created us and could destroy us just as easily—brandishing a weapon in front of us that would essentially shut our bodies down. I remembered my first scent of female hormones as one of us began to change and how I had turned into an animal, and my brothers had to hold me back. I had been the first one to lose control like that. I was the weakest, and I didn't want to be weak. I should be protecting Tori.

"You don't understand." I forced the words through gritted teeth.

I wasn't weak. I *wasn't*.

"Take me, Vitri. It's okay, I trust you. Please take me." When I didn't answer, she pushed herself onto her toes and planted a hand on my shoulder, whispering against my ear, "Fuck me, Vitri."

I lost control.

The roar that escaped my throat was foreign to me, and I ripped my loin cloth from my body and pounced at Tori. She cried out in surprise but didn't struggle or try to move away, instead remaining supple and soft in my hands as I lowered her to the ground. Grunting, I began grinding my erect cock against the inside of her thigh, barely enough awareness in me left to check that she was wet. Tracing a greedy palm down her body, I slipped a finger into her waiting cunt, and she cried out again, arching her back and pressing herself against me. She was wet, so deliciously wet and ready for me. Sucking her taste off my finger, I lined up my cock with her entrance, using my hands to spread her thighs and hold her legs apart. Her scent hit me, and I released a snarl. Tori reached up and grabbed my arms, gripping me with her fingers and talking to me. I pushed the haze in my mind aside to hear her—she was encouraging me.

Begging me.

"Vitri, please. Come on, fuck me, please. Please."

With a groan, I slid my cock into her waiting cunt, her moans only enticing me to push harder until I was completely enveloped within her. She was so tight around me, and I twitched and groaned as she clenched. Glancing down, I watched where our bodies met, her legs parted, and her cunt stretched open to take me.

I growled out her name, gripped her hips, and pulled out slightly, only to slam back into her.

Her encouraging moans broke whatever was left of my control.

Planting a fist next to her head, I kept my other hand gripped on her hip. I leaned over Tori and fucked into her at a ruthless pace. I didn't want to hurt her, but I couldn't stop, and her cries increased in pitch the harder and faster I took her. She took everything I had to give, opening up to me and eventually wrapping one of her legs around my waist.

Soon, a thin sheen of sweat covered her brow and chest, and her moans became whimpers.

"Make yourself come," I said, not slowing down.

Tori didn't question and lowered her hand between our bodies, rubbing herself, the tips of her fingers brushing against my cock with every inward thrust. The sounds she made took on a different edge as she drew closer to her peak, and I kept going until I felt her clench around me harder and cry out my name, the sound so sweet I roared again.

Grabbing her hips, I moved, and she shrieked as I stood, still inside her, and cupped her ass in my palms. Tori was so small, so delicate, but she took everything from me as I pumped her against me, using her delicious cunt to milk the cum from me. I was so close and moved faster, needing to fill her with my seed, desperate to breed her, to make her mine in every way.

Tori's eyes were squeezed shut, and there was a pang in my chest, hoping I wasn't hurting her, but unable to find the control to slow, not when I was so close. With a shudder and final thrust, I came, pumping my cum into her and groaning at how she moaned at the sensation.

Lowering to the ground, I kept Tori on my lap, cradled her against my body, and kept my twitching cock inside her.

CHAPTER 21

TORI

It *had* been a good plan I thought as I sat on Vitri's lap with his cock still hard inside me while we came down from our respective highs. It *was* a good plan—I hadn't changed my mind about that.

Vitri's state of mind had deteriorated throughout the day, but no matter how much he seemed to change, his desire to care for and protect me never wavered. If he could put my well-being above his own, then I wanted to help him in any way I could. The fact that being fucked by Vitri was incredibly pleasurable was simply a bonus, and as I traced my fingers down his cheek and waited for him to look me in the eyes, I sighed with contentment.

Vitri's eyes snapped open, still blazing with lust, the look so intense I recoiled slightly. Then he grinned, and I got a glimpse of the Vitri I knew.

Before his expression darkened again, his hands gripped my ass as he lifted me slightly, slowly rocking me up and down his cock.

"Again," he grunted out.

"Wh-what?"

He jutted his hips up, thrusting his still-hard cock deep into me, growling when I cried out. "*Again.*"

"Vitri..." I licked my lips, my mouth suddenly dry. "I ah, I'll need to come again. I don't think I'm wet enough."

He said nothing more, only snarled and pulled me from his lap, slamming me against the ground hard enough to knock the air from my lungs. His vice-like grip on my hips shifted to my thighs as he spread my legs in front of him and dove between them, hungrily lapping and sucking at my clit.

"Oh *fuck!*" I cried out. Unprepared for the sudden attention and still sensitive, it was a matter of seconds before I felt my peak build again. Vitri grumbled his approval as I twitched against him, gripping his head and holding his face between my legs, grinding into his mouth as that magnificent curve of his tongue cupped my clit with every lick. He was relentless, determined to make me come hard and fast, and I had no chance of doing anything but.

When I came, he drove his tongue into me, working the curl of it against my G-spot as he lapped up my juices. When I began to see stars, the sensations became too much. He removed his tongue from me, and with a strong hand, he flipped me onto my stomach, crushing me under his weight as he penetrated me from behind.

"Fuck!" My hands gripped the soil and moss of the woodland floor as Vitri placed a palm on my abdomen, lifting my hips slightly to meet his thrusts halfway and resuming his previous relentless pace.

The winds began to pick up as he fucked me into the ground, and I wanted to alert him, to remind him we needed to find shelter. But as I turned my head, his expression was animalistic, pure instinct driving him to take me. Nothing else mattered. Nothing else would penetrate his consciousness in this moment, and I ducked my head against the cold as he kept going.

It was sensation overload, every inch of him hitting every part of me that was already overstimulated, and I felt constantly on the edge of another release.

"Touch my clit," I said, hoping he had enough awareness left in him to follow through.

He was silent aside from the grunts of pleasure and exertion for a few moments before I felt a brush against my clit. His hands still gripped my hips, tilting me up to meet his thrusts but not quite pulling me to my knees. His vines traced along the inside of my thighs, a delicate touch that ended by clamping me in place as they worked against my clit. I cried out, shuddering through another orgasm, drawn out by the pleasure of being stretched to my limit by Vitri and the primal way he took me.

The vines continued to work against me, and my protests were lost as the wind picked up again, howling between the trees and almost drowning out Vitri's roar as he came again, pumping his cum into me as the vines worked me toward another mind-bending orgasm that had me collapsing to the ground. Vitri pulled his cock from me, and I groaned as he wrapped me in his arms and rolled over so I was cradled between his large body and a gathering of thin tree trunks. Vitri repositioned himself so he was taking the brunt of the winds, and I was protected.

I was too exhausted to protest, instead falling asleep to the sound of his heart rate returning to normal.

A gentle vibration rumbled against my back, and I awoke to find Vitri still pressed against me, his heavy arm draped over my body as he held me close. Wiggling against him, I tried to loosen his grip, stopping when he groaned.

He was still hard.

Okay, so maybe this plan was backfiring.

We wouldn't get anywhere if Vitri needed to fuck like he did last night several times a day. As much as it felt fucking incredible, I'm hoping he had enough willpower to keep himself controlled until we reached camp every night at the very least. Another day and we should be nearing the ocean, then it would be maybe one more day to move along the coast until we were parallel with the base of the mountains.

But between our descent to the beach and the mountains, our task would be locating the pod. Erica seemed sure she had seen one move toward the ocean, but her certainty had waned each time we discussed it, and I understood her hesitancy.

I'd touched her arm. "I'm not going to hold you personally responsible if the pod isn't *exactly* where you suspect it would be." She'd bitten her lip, staring out toward the ocean as if hoping for a glimpse of it, so I continued, "We were all in a panic, and the fact you had managed to keep track of the pods at all was better than I had done."

I'd walk this island for as long as it took to find

the others.

Vitri groaned again, wrapped his arm tighter around me, and crushed me against his chest. I squirmed against his hold. "Hey," I cried and slapped his arm gently. When he didn't stir, I tried again, louder and harder, and he jolted awake.

"Are you okay?" His tone was laced with concern, and I was relieved but also a bit disappointed the animalistic growls had subsided.

"I'm fine." He buried his face in the crook of my neck, inhaling deeply before he huffed out a contented breath that left me squirming at the tickling sensation against my neck. "Let me go, I need to get up."

He did so reluctantly and stood after I did, stretching his long arms toward the sky and rumbling out a loud groan which ended in a growl. Glancing down, he smirked and searched for his discarded loin cloth.

After I'd been to the bathroom, dressed, and had some water, I picked up some leftover food from the previous night and handed a piece to Vitri. "How are you feeling?"

He pressed his lips together, looking uncertain. "Better, my mind is clearer." His gaze wandered my body, and a shudder worked its way down his spine. "But the urges are still there. I can only hope they won't get stronger throughout the day until I lose control again."

It was my turn to smirk. "That wouldn't be so bad. We can always satiate you again tonight."

A jumble of emotions played across his face. "Are you sore?"

My thighs clenched together at his words, and he noticed the movement, frowning. "A little bit, but I'm okay. It's more a dull ache." I held up my hand when he went to protest. "But it's a good ache... trust me."

Vitri shook his head. "I should be in better control than this. I'm sorry."

"You admitted that you've not had this reaction before. So it might take you a bit to figure out how to control it. That's okay... we'll figure it out together."

He lunged at me, scooped me up in his arms, and spun me. When he stopped, his breath was hot against my ear, and I could feel the smile curling his lips. "And in the meantime, I can fuck you until you come around my cock. Every. Single. Night."

I shuddered and was unable to contain the squeak that escaped my lips. Vitri looked much too pleased with himself as a flush crept across my cheeks. When he placed me back on my feet, I frowned and huffed at him, hoping my cheeks weren't quite as red as they felt, the heat practically burning from me.

"Let's get moving," I said, clearing my throat as Vitri continued to grin at me.

Smug asshole.

We collected our water bags and spears and started walking.

CHAPTER
22

VITRI

As we walked, Tori asked again about the planet and animal species we encountered, wanting to know which were introduced, which were native, and which females were brought to the planet with the same fate as her. If we passed a species, I identified as kidnapped from their home planet, and if they were alone, Tori fretted, and I wasn't able to hold the truth from her.

"When you showed me the asha, there were four of them." I hummed but didn't respond, resuming my pace as Tori trotted to keep up. "And me and the girls, there are four of us." When I still didn't respond, she grabbed my hand and held it as we walked. "So that species we just passed…"

"Furnia." The yellowish tinge to their skin would still be visible if I turned and looked, two of their four arms clinging to the tree trunks as if ready to fling themselves into action and run.

"Right," Tori said, clearly not letting me off the hook with this one. "There were only two, and another species we saw earlier today was alone. Where are the others?"

Grinding my teeth, I tried not to look at her because I didn't want to see her face when I told her the ugly truth, unable to lie to her. "The Ghaal might have gotten to them."

Tori stopped dead. I took another two steps before I also stopped and turned to face her. *"Might?"*

"Sometimes we don't get to them in time, Tori." I ran my hands down my face, not wanting to relive the reminders of all the species I had failed to save. "Some of them we can't communicate with as we can't get close enough to learn their language." She took a few steps to come level with me and ran her small palm down my arm as I whispered, "We can't save them all."

"Do they…" Tori's throat worked as she swallowed heavily. "Do they ever come back?"

Whatever guilt that bubbled in my stomach

cemented as agonizing pain dragged through my body and reminded me of all those I had failed. Sometimes, I wished we had stayed with the Ghaal, then at least they would never have turned their attention to other species and begun this ridiculous campaign to kidnap and steal. But if we helped them breed, then what? There would be more of them, with our DNA mixed in, and they would be stronger, faster, smarter, and who knows what damage they would do then.

It was a cyclic conundrum to which there was no correct answer.

"I'm sorry," Tori whispered when I didn't answer her question, knowing my silence meant *no* because they didn't come back. None of them did. Not ever. If the Ghaal were unable to impregnate them through *traditional* means, they would attempt surgery. Failing that, the species would be experimented on to see if any part of them could be transplanted or used to save the Ghaal.

"It's not your fault... you didn't know," I said.

"It's not your fault either," she said, and I grunted, a sound neither of agreement nor acceptance.

We walked in silence for a while longer before Tori broke it. "Did you have sex with one of the asha?"

The question caught me off guard, and despite my earlier brooding, I barked out a laugh. When I glanced at Tori, her cheeks were aflame with embarrassment and anger. "Are you jealous, my mate?"

Mate.

The term had slipped out, and it was too late to take back what I said. Tori stuttered and stammered through a few responses before ultimately deciding to disregard that part of the sentence. "I'm not jealous," she said.

I raised my eyebrows at her, wiggling them when she glared at me again, and I didn't bother fighting to keep the grin from my face. "Oh no?"

Her spine stiffened, and she pressed forward with her questioning. "Did you, though?"

Stopping, I took a step and spun on the ball of my foot, forcing Tori to stop so she didn't walk straight into me. Crouching in front of her, I ran my hands up and down her arms, a satisfied growl rumbling through my chest at how she shuddered under my touch.

My mate.

"No, Tori. I didn't have sex with any of the asha. It's been a long, long time since I have done anything of the sort before you, and it's *only* you that brings out the instinct in me."

I loved this jealous side of her as much as I loved how she was strong and willing to fight, the part of her that had hunted for herself her first day on a strange planet. But Tori needed reassurance from *me,* and I would tell her over and over again as many times as she needed to hear it.

My pheromones pumped out stronger, and her eyelids fluttered for a moment as she held my gaze, her expression softening. I wanted to take her here and now. I wanted the freedom to push her onto the ground whenever I needed her and sink my cock into her waiting cunt. My shoulders stiffened as I caught the thoughts before they got too far and tried to squash them down under layers of control.

Later.

There would be time for that later.

Was I so weak that even giving into my urges wasn't enough to control me?

"I don't even know why I'm jealous," she whispered, and I brushed my thumb across her cheek, my grin only widened further as her eyes narrowed at me.

"Because you like me, and you just can't admit it?"

She laughed as I smirked, my smile and her chuckle fading together as we both realized at the same time it was true. Her pupils flickered between mine, so much emotion in her brown eyes. She hid behind her veil of snark, the way she talked and fought with every step.

But inside, did she crave a mate as I did?

Tori cleared her throat. "We should keep moving, cover as much ground before nightfall."

I smiled and took her hand because she had given me hope and gave me more hope with every passing moment. Her attitude around me had already softened, and when we touched, it was more than touch alone—we connected.

She was my mate, and I would wait a lifetime for her to realize it too.

"Whatever you say, my mate," I said, taking a bold leap and purposefully throwing the term out there. Tori's fingers twitched in mine, and she glanced sideways at me.

But she didn't pull away, instead giving my hand a small squeeze.

My heart leaped in my chest.

We set up camp near the edge of the woodlands, and I think Tori was glad to see a change in terrain. From here, the trees would thin and give way to thick shrubbery and sandy soil. The shrubs were harsh and would cut into Tori's delicate skin, and again, I cursed myself for not making her a pair of suitable pants. She would have to tread carefully because I'm certain she wouldn't allow me to carry her.

I grinned at the idea—she wouldn't allow it

without a fight anyway. Maybe I'd have to throw her over my shoulder until we reached the cliffs.

Which we would by late afternoon tomorrow. Then we'd follow it along until we could find a safe way down to the beach. I hoped that the vantage point of the cliff might show us the location of the Moek unit before we descended. Otherwise, we would have to search the beach simply hoping we located it or signs of life.

Perhaps we would find my brother, Sahcor, first, who had taken up residence in the area.

My skin crawled. While we were far enough away from the Ghaal community to be safe, we were closer than I was comfortable with, and I don't know how Ilk stood to be as close as he was at the base of the mountains.

Sitting Tori in my lap, which she protested only slightly by trying to squirm away and huffing out an amused breath when I wrapped my arms around her and held her still, I discussed my thoughts with her. If she were to stay with me and be my mate, we needed to work together as a team.

"I think we need to head straight for Sahcor rather than search for the unit."

"What's a Sahcor?"

"Sahcor is another of my brothers who lives on the beach on this side of the island."

"Another brother? What does he look like?"

I shrugged, keeping my arms around Tori. "I

don't know."

She turned slightly and looked at me over her shoulder. "How can you not know?"

"You forget, Tori. We are an adaptive species. Left long enough in an environment, we'll change to survive and be part of it. Which is why Ilk looked like the mountains, and I look like the forest."

"So Sahcor is going to be some sort of water nymph?"

"I don't know what that is."

She laughed. "Neither do I, really." She gently played with the vines that wrapped around my arms, rolling them between her fingers and almost eliciting a purr from me. I tightened my hold on her, unable to help myself. I'd have to remind her that the vines are part of me, and I can feel them as though they were a limb. Her touching me like that was nothing short of foreplay, and while I had felt my instincts rising again during the day, I had mostly been able to maintain control.

After a pause, she added, "What about my friend?"

"We'll find her," I soothed, inhaling the scent of her hair at the nape of her neck and regretting it instantly when my arousal spiked. "Sahcor would have sought out the unit. Find Sahcor, find your friend."

Tori relaxed into my hold, at least partially satiated with the news her friend would be safe with Sahcor.

My cock twitched under my loin cloth, and I almost groaned.

Was Tori safe with me?

I stood abruptly, and Tori dropped to the ground, crying out, "Hey!" As I took a few steps away, she scrambled to her feet and rounded on me. "What was that for?"

"You feel too good. I don't want to lose control again."

Her hands were on her hips, one tilted higher than the other as she pouted, and I almost smirked. "In case you hadn't noticed, I got off when you lost control on me. I don't understand why you're fighting this so hard. You were so much better today than you were yesterday. Maybe all we need to do is let you unleash until you learn to control it."

"It's not enough, though!"

My shout startled her, and I was filled with shame and regret when she dropped her hands to her sides and leaned away from me. "What do you mean it's not enough? Do you mean me? Am I not enough?"

"No, no. That's not what I mean." I ran a hand over my head. How to explain to her that the urges have been building from the moment we woke this morning? Tori was enough, *more* than enough. But with the thoughts that infiltrated my mind every time I looked at her, I was beginning to fear these instincts wouldn't be satiated until she was pregnant with my child. I was designed to *breed,* not just *fuck.* But she was still coming to terms with being on this planet, let alone being with someone alien to her—someone like me. I could read her hesitations by how she went quiet and hugged her arms around herself, always after I asked her questions about her home planet or culture. She'd answer happily, then go quiet and remain so for a while after. Tori missed her home, but she couldn't go back. It wasn't fair of me to simply tell her to get over it and come to me as my mate. I needed to win her over but not only with sex.

I wanted her to *want* me, to *need* me, and not just for survival.

It was too many emotions all at once—things I hadn't felt or even thought about in years while living alone. I wasn't lying when I told her no other species had brought this out in me, and it had been so long since I lived with the other Synths, I couldn't even say for sure if I'd ever felt this way around them. We weren't together long enough for some of us to change gender fully in order to allow breeding. My brothers and I developed a bond as a family, and we didn't give that time to change and adapt before we left the Ghaal. We weren't related, not really, created with a mixture of synthetic and a random selection of Ghaal DNA. Biologically, Synths were perfectly capable of mating with each other, which was the whole idea of our creation.

But I didn't want that. I wanted Tori and for her to feel the same and not because she had no other choice.

"Talk to me." Tori took a step closer, raising a hand to touch me, although a frown was still present on her forehead, creasing her gorgeous skin as she tried to figure out what was going on.

I couldn't even be sure myself. I was figuring it out as I went and didn't want her to have to deal with everything that came with that.

"I'm sorry." It was all I could think to say—there was so much else on my mind.

"Don't be sorry, just..." she reached out and touched my arm, and when I didn't protest, she moved closer and laid her palms on my chest. "Talk to me. We can figure it out together."

Her scent was intoxicating, and while I thought I had the strength in me to fight it, I was *almost* certain I could maintain control for another day...

I wasn't sure I wanted to, though.

CHAPTER 23

TORI

Vitri grabbed me then, pulled me close to him, and hungrily inhaled the scent of my hair. I wanted to tell him to stop, partially because we needed to talk this out, and God knows I was never one for sitting down and having deep and meaningful conversations. But he was struggling, and the idiot had grown on me, and I *cared* about his big, dumb, grinning face. I also wanted to push him away because I hadn't been able to bathe properly in days and was sure I smelled like sweat and dirt. But Vitri couldn't seem to get enough of me, and his hand dropped down and lifted my tunic. His velvety skin ran against my thighs as I opened my legs to welcome his touch. It took more of my willpower than I wanted to admit not to gyrate my hips and beg him to touch me already.

God, why did he have to smell *so fucking good?*

Right, the pheromones. I remembered.

But beyond that, I still wanted him, and I was done fighting it. Because this entire situation and my simply *being* here on this planet was a *lot* to take in. It turned out Erica had been right—*fuck it.* Do what we want because what do we have to lose? I looked forward to reuniting with Erica once we found the others. It seemed she was more my kind of person than I'd realized.

Vitri and I moaned together as he pushed a finger inside me, then another, and my legs trembled as he began pumping them in and out. As my arousal increased, the sounds of him fingering me became wet and loud, my readiness for him on full display. He wrapped an arm around my waist, holding still when I wasn't sure I could hold myself up for much longer.

He had that animalistic look in his eyes again, his pupils blown out, and I brushed my fingers down his face. He *trembled*. If I saw him on Earth, I would swear he was a monster, and here he was, trembling under my touch while he pleasured me.

"You don't have to control yourself, Vitri, not with me."

Something flashed in his eyes, something akin to regret, and his fingers stilled inside me before he withdrew his hand. Rejection washed over me, replaced by anger, and when I slapped my palms to his chest, ready to push him away, he wrapped his arms around me and crushed me close to him. This on-again-off-again bullshit was killing me, as if I didn't already have enough to deal with. What with being on an alien planet with one sexy alien and several murdery-rapey ones.

"Let me go," I protested, wiggling against his hold even though I knew it was useless. If he didn't want me to move, I wouldn't be able to move. But Vitri had never held me against my will before, always letting me go when I demanded it. "Let me go," I repeated.

If he didn't want me, then I didn't want him either.

Yeah, you keep telling yourself that.

His green eyes studied me, and I stopped fighting him. He looked *hurt.*

Vitri was the one rejecting *me.* After fighting for my affection this entire time, I finally gave into him fully, he turned me away and stopped touching me. So what did he have to be hurt about?

"I want you to want me," he mumbled.

His confession caught me off guard, and I stilled.

Tilting back slightly, I worked my arms up between us so I could grab his face and make him look at me when he didn't do it on his own. This alien, with his deep green skin, bright eyes, and vines that were part of his body—his impossibly big body that made me feel safe and turned me on like crazy—I *did* want him. For some bullshit reason or another, I actually *did.* I'd missed his cheekiness when he receded from me the other day, and now I'd glimpsed having him back. The realization of how much I'd craved our back-and-forth was like a punch in the gut. He was that perfect line between challenging me and looking after me.

I didn't want to lose him again, but he kept pulling away from me.

"I *do* want you, you big idiot," I said, brushing my lips against his. Instead of seeing a grin as I hoped, his lips turned down in sadness as he ran his fingers up and down my back, almost absentmindedly.

"I want you to want me..." He made a choking sound which edged with a growl. "Not just because of the sex."

That was what he was worried about? That I only liked him because he was good at fucking?

My green-skinned, forest-giant... *insecure* alien man.

Of all the things...

I shook my head, smiling to myself. "How can you be so stupid and so smart at the same time?"

A frown creased his forehead. "That's not possible."

I tapped his head with my fingertip. "Evidently it is, you big lug." When he continued to frown, his eyes still full of uncertainly and fear, I sighed. "I *do* like you, Vitri, and I want to be with you because I like you. The sex is just a bonus, okay? I want to be with *you.*"

I expected him to smile or, at the very least, smirk at me in that way he does, but he continued to study my face. When I went to lift my hand to his cheek again, he snatched at my wrist before I made contact. As I opened my mouth to ask what the problem was, he leaned forward, dragged me against him, and pressed his tongue into my mouth. Soon, the kiss became urgent, and that rumbling growl started in his chest, settling into almost a purr when I began rubbing my hands against the huge flat expanse of his muscles. "Do you need to release again?"

His hips were rocking a rhythm against me that was already answering my question, and I chuckled quietly. What I wouldn't have given to have someone like Vitri back home. Beyond the sex— although that was mind-blowing, and I certainly wasn't complaining—but someone who made me feel like he did.

Were my feelings for Vitri, whatever they were, enough to stop me from missing a home I couldn't go back to? Maybe not, but it was a hell of a compensation.

Vitri pulled away from the kiss when I stopped moving my lips against his, gripped my chin, and forced me to look at him. The scent of his pheromones was heavy in the air, and his erection pressed against me, shifting his loin cloth to the side until it was practically useless. "Are you okay?" he asked.

In response, I grabbed his cock, unable to ignore it any longer, and stroked his length in my hands. Vitri threw his head back and groaned, thrusting his hips to meet the motion of my hands, precum dripping from the large head. I wanted to taste him.

When I dropped to my knees, Vitri reached down to grab me, and I laughed, batting his hands away. "I didn't fall, Vitri. Let me do this for you."

When I circled my tongue around the head of his cock, his eyes widened for a moment before he clamped them shut, the rumbling of the growl through his chest intensifying. He tasted the same as his vines did when he put them in my mouth—earthy and musky. His precum was sticky, thicker than humans', and coated the inside of my mouth when I took the head of his cock between my lips. I kept my hands moving up and down his shaft, turning them as I pumped his cock, flicking my tongue along the odd texture of the skin on the head.

With a roar, Vitri grabbed my head and thrust forward into my mouth, and I slapped my hands against his thighs until he pulled out.

"I'm sorry, I'm sorry," he repeated, his voice strained.

"It's okay." I smirked up at him, still on my knees, and wiped my mouth on the back of my hand. "I love the taste of your cock."

That was apparently too much for him, and with another roar, he was on me, crushing me against the ground and grinding his hard length between my legs, hitting my clit with every forward thrust. "Going to make you come against my cock, Tori," he crooned, his voice shifting into another growl as he finished the sentence. He cradled my head in his giant hands as he continued to thrust against me. "Then I'm going to fuck you. Is that okay?"

"Yes..." I arched my back, shifting my hips to meet his thrusts as the ridges on his cock stimulated my clit. He didn't relent, pushing me toward my climax, his mouth meeting the crook of my neck and shoulder and nibbling, licking, biting, pulling me closer to the edge. I gripped his ass with my fingernails when pleasure surged through me, and he stilled as I rocked myself against him, drawing out my orgasm.

"See?" I panted, wiping the sweat from my brow, "You're getting better at controlling yourself every day. You stopped moving."

He purred at my approval, but his eyes were still animalistic, darkened with the widening of his pupils as he shifted his hips to line himself up with my pussy. He slowly pushed in, and I moaned as the head penetrated me. Then with a snarl, he thrust forward, bottoming out inside me with one swift motion.

"Fuck, *Vitri.*"

"I love it when you say my name. Going to make you scream it."

The slick drag of his cock inside me drove me to the edge of pleasure with every thrust, and he kept his arms around me as I lay on the ground, protecting me from the outside world even as he fucked me into the soil. When I wrapped my legs around his hips, his growling increased again, and with his chest so close, it was all I could hear. His thrusts became erratic, harder, and deeper as he chased his own high. Vitri's head dropped against my shoulder again, and I could hear him muttering over the growling.

"My mate..."

He repeated it over and over as he reached his peak. When the pleasure hit him, and he was shoved hard over the edge, releasing his warm cum inside me, I gripped his shoulders as he cried out the words, roaring them above the sound of his growls.

My lips curled into a smile against his chest as he

collapsed on top of me.
His *mate?*
I didn't mind the sound of that.

CHAPTER 24

VITRI

For our morning meal before setting off toward the most treacherous part of our journey—not only because of the proximity of the Ghaal colony but because even if we found a suitable place to scale the cliffside to the beach, it wouldn't be easy—Tori insisted on attempting to hunt for herself. Once again, I admired her streak of stubbornness and independence, and my desire for her was only fueled more when I attempted to drag her into my lap and touch her.

She wiggled out of my grasp and stood. "I need to

learn to hunt, and *you* need to practice control."

She was right, but I wasn't going to tell her that. "Don't you like it when I lose control on you?"

Tori cupped my face, grinned at my smirk, and planted a chaste kiss on my lips. I could smell her arousal, though. She got wet at simply the *idea* of being mated by me, and pride only served to make me smile more. "You know I do, but we have work to do, which means we need to eat first."

"Fine." I stood, slapping Tori sharply on the ass as she moved away from me. She squealed and shoved at me but laughed as well. I loved the sound of her laughter. It seemed to be happening more often now. The only thing I liked more was the sounds she made when I made her come.

Tori picked up her spear after taking a drink. I told her to bring the water bag with her, and we'll find a place to refill it while we look for something to hunt. I hadn't been down to the edge of the island in many years, but the sound of trickling water was on the peripheral of my hearing, so there needed to be something close.

Where there was water, there were animals.

I debated teasing Tori about the asha being near the water supply just to make her jealous again. But she was holding a spear with a look of determination plastered on her perfect face, and I decided to save that particular tease for later. The fact that she had been *jealous* over me was thrilling, and it made me feel good. It didn't surprise me it was the asha and not any other species that had drawn that out of her. They were beautiful, and evidently evolved to attract males. Perhaps the same things that drew males to them also made females weary. Even though Tori had been initially drawn to their song just as I had when they first arrived, she was still jealous.

For me.

Now may not be the right time to tease her so soon, but that wouldn't stop me from using it against her in the future. If only to see her cheeks flush and her little hands curl into fists at the indignation of my mere suggestion that she was *jealous.*

Heading toward the sound of water, I kept my gaze low to search for tracks of signs of wildlife around the area. There were many, but only one I recognized.

Swooping my gaze upward toward the sky, I squinted through the haze of the rising sun and waited. It was early morning, and they would be feeding soon before sleeping for the day.

If Tori wanted a challenge, I'd give her one.

And maybe a part of me liked it when she needed me.

Pointing upward as a shadow passed over us, Tori followed my gaze. "Vultures?" she asked.

"Volti."

Tori shaded her eyes with a hand on her forehead. "It looks like a vulture." She then glanced at me. "Is *that* what you want me to hunt?"

"Yes."

She offered me a sideways glance, her eyes narrowing with suspicion. "Why do I feel like you're setting me up for failure?" My smile faltered just for a moment as I was caught out in my game. Tori jumped on the spot and pointed her finger at me. "Ah-ha! You *are* trying to set me up. What's the matter? Don't like the idea that I can fend for myself?" My jaw tensed as I ground my teeth together, hating that she could read me so easily. Her expression changed, softening, although the smirk remained. "Oh my God, that's it, isn't it? You're worried if I learn to hunt and forage, I won't need you."

I started to regret not teasing her about the asha when I had the chance.

Tori grabbed my wrist and yanked until I bent at the hips so we were face to face. "How many times am I going to have to tell you I'm with *you?*" I simply held her gaze, not trusting myself to speak. With a slight shove, she let go of my face, her grin back in place. "That is unless you piss me off. Now, let's get some food." She shoved my arm playfully. "Feed me... your mate is hungry."

Tori giggled at the rumble that surged in my chest at hearing her use the word *mate*, and I managed a smile. The past few days had been tumultuous. I'd gone from being a protector and a guardian, to finding the personality and side of me I had forgotten, to being overrun with desire to the point of being barely more than an animal until it all left me feeling uncertain of myself and everything I did.

All I really knew for sure anymore is that I wanted Tori. I wanted her to stay and be *with* me. She said she wanted the same thing, but she would still pine for her home planet.

I only hoped I was enough for her.

Setting a challenge to Tori to hunt a volti wasn't something she was willing to back down from, and I should've known. We waited longer than we should have for one of them to settle for its feed, and at least she allowed me to assist her in lining up the angle for her spear. Standing behind her with my arms wrapped around hers, guiding her, felt so good I almost took her again right there.

But she was right—my mate needed to eat.

She threw the spear and missed but not by much.

Ready to take the kill, I threw my larger spear a split second later, connecting with the volti's chest and sending it tumbling back to the ground after it moved to take off to the sky again.

"Bullshit!" Tori cried out, and I smiled. I couldn't tell if she was angry she had missed or impressed I hadn't, but either way, her insistence on using language to ease her frustrations amused me.

"You did well," I said as we moved to collect the kill. I began cleaning the carcass on our way back to where we had a collection of wood, ready to make a small fire. "You were so close." She huffed air out through her nose, said nothing, and I chuckled again. "It takes practice."

Still, she said nothing but glared at me when I laughed again.

This only made me laugh more. I loved her little tantrums.

"One day," she said, using her hands to help propel herself over a large stone. "I'll be a better hunter than you."

"I look forward to it. Then *you* can look after *me.*"

Her smile was coy, but she said nothing as we reached our temporary camp and began the fire. After cooking the meat, I made certain Tori was full before I ate. Our next part of the journey would be difficult, and she needed her strength.

We would find Sahcor. The sooner, the better because the sooner we found Tori's friends and she saw they were safe, the sooner I could have her all to myself again.

TORI

"Talk to me."

I needed some form of distraction because the easiest way down the side of the cliff face to the beach was apparently a steep-as-hell wall. It was practically amateur rock climbing, facing the wall and working our way downward by finding nooks and footholds we could use. Vitri wrapped his vines around my waist and promised me he wouldn't let me fall.

I believed him, but it was still difficult to concentrate.

"Are you afraid of heights?" he asked.

"No," I said, a squeal escaping my lips as the rocks slipped under my fingers. Vitri's vines tightened around my waist, and it was comforting but not enough. "I'm not afraid of heights as such. I handled your treehouse just fine." I glanced down. "I'm afraid of being impaled on spikey rocks, though."

"I won't let you fall."

I sighed, taking a few steps sideways on the narrow ridge to find another hold. "Talk to me anyway so I'm distracted."

"Tell me about your home."

"Too vague, Vitri. Ask me something specific."

"Did you have a mate?"

I laughed out loud, managing a few more descending steps without fear while laughing at the growl that rumbled through his chest at my response or my lack of response. It was difficult not to laugh, especially after the hard time he'd given *me* about jealousy. "No need to be jealous, Vitri. At least *my* potential suitors are galaxies away." I remembered the asha and the way they had called with a seductive song. Scowling, I added, "Yours still sing to you."

"I regret showing you the asha."

"I regret not punching their beautiful alien faces in," I mumbled.

Vitri chuckled before continuing, "You didn't

answer my question."

"I had an ex... mate." It sounded such an odd way to say it. "Boyfriend... we call them boyfriends and girlfriends or partners. So, I had an ex-boyfriend."

"Do you miss him?"

I thought for a moment. "No, not him. I miss home, though. I miss my mother, even though she probably doesn't miss me."

"Why wouldn't she miss you?"

"She doesn't remember me."

Vitri's brow furrowed as he waited for me to climb on a flat surface next to him. When I got my footing, he placed his hands on my hips to steady me. "I don't understand."

I looked away, willing the tears to stay at bay and hating that they rose so readily simply because I'd spoken about her out loud rather than keeping her safe, locked in my private thoughts. "Sometimes, when humans get old, they lose their memory. It's just one of those shitty things that happens."

"Why does it happen?"

"I don't know," I sighed the words out. While this conversation was working to distract me, I was hating all the emotions it was stirring in my chest. "But it's probably hereditary."

The second the words left my lips, I regretted it. There was a brief silence as Vitri processed what I had said, and I grunted as I was yanked forward against his chest. "Will you forget me?" His voice sounded strained, and it pulled at something in my chest.

Wrapping my arms around him, I squeezed slightly. I was never one to lie purely to soothe the feelings of others—it just didn't come naturally. But Vitri *cared* about me for reasons I had yet to place, and I didn't want to torture him with something that may never happen. "No," I said, leaning into his hold. "I'll never forget you."

There was another pause, and I'm sure Vitri knew I was lying. When he released me, he offered a grin. "If you do forget me, I'll simply remind you every day."

"Deal." I shyly returned his smile before he guided me to move to his left as I was to follow him down again. When my foot slipped, and I gasped, I bit my tongue too late to stop the sound of panic that escaped. I needed to keep talking to keep up the distraction. It was a bonus that I enjoyed talking to Vitri, but I wouldn't let him know just how much. It would increase his already over-inflated ego.

"Did you ever have a job?" I asked.

"I don't think so, not unless you count being created to breed a job."

"So you just spend all day doing whatever you want?" He didn't answer immediately, and something dark passed over his eyes when I glanced at him. I regretted my question. I should've known it would take him back to his time with the

Ghaal and whatever they had done to him and his brothers. Vitri had ghosted his hands over my calves as he guided me where to step, and I added, "I mean, since you left. You just do whatever?"

"I guess so. Aside from protecting introduced species."

"Aliens like me."

He chuckled, moving his hand up to grab my ass and squeezed. "There are no aliens like you."

Why did my mind keep flooding back to the images of the asha? Them and their stupidly gorgeous skin that almost glowed and their bullshit songs they sang to lure Vitri to them.

Oh, dear God, I *was* jealous.

This seemed like a moment I should be standing in front of a mirror and proclaiming, *who are you? I don't recognize the woman in front of me. You used to be cool, man.*

I guess being abducted by aliens and dumped on a strange planet changes your perspective.

"Your turn," I said, ignoring the ache in my fingers as I gripped a particularly sharp edge.

"For what?"

"To ask me a question. Keep talking to me."

"Soon you can relax, mate... we are almost at the beach."

His soothing tone sent a rush through me that was both calming and thrilling. He had started calling me *mate* more often, and I still didn't mind it. Maybe it was almost his version of *babe,* and it was cute. I nodded. "Ask me something else about Earth."

"What was your favorite food?"

My lips twisted in thought as I considered the question. If I had to pick one thing, *only one,* it wasn't as easy as just saying *chocolate* or *coffee.* Though, fuck knows, I would kill for a coffee. I made a noise of consideration so Vitri knew I had heard his question and was probably putting way more thought into it than necessary as we continued to climb.

"Duck," I finally said.

"Duck?"

"It's a bird, a flying animal, kind of like your vulture things but smaller. My mom used to cook duck with orange sauce... a fruit... and marinate it. It was mouth-watering. So fucking good." I sighed. "Kinda hard to realize I'll never have it again."

"I'll find you some duck and orange," Vitri proclaimed, wrapping his hands around my waist and lifting me from the cliff face.

I chuckled before sighing deeply as I felt my feet slightly sink into the sand.

We made it, finally. "How? There are no ducks on this planet."

Vitri wrapped an arm around me and scooped me up, spinning on the spot. "We will try every animal and fruit on the planet until we find one that tastes the same. We'll journey across the complete island, even if it takes several cycles, and we'll find you some *duck.*"

"And coffee?"

"Coffee?"

I laughed. "Never mind. Now, put me down. You're very cute, but I'm getting dizzy, and we have to find your brother."

Vitri didn't put me down, instead taking a moment to stare into my eyes, the green of his glowing as a cheeky grin lit his face. "You think I'm cute?"

Laughing, I slapped his chest lightly. "Put me *down.*"

He did, and it was difficult not to smile as he continued to smirk and took my hand in his, squeezing slightly as he led me toward the water. Glancing backward, the cliff face seemed even more imposing looking up at it, and I was floored we'd manage to climb down relatively unscathed, save for a few scratches. Wiggling my hand free from his, I unhooked the water bag from his shoulder and took a grateful swig before offering it back.

We stopped a few yards from where the ocean splashed against the shore. From the escape pod, it had looked so similar to Earth, save for the color— a deep gray, almost like dirty water from a mop bucket. The waves crashed and fell the same way they did back home, leaving trails of off-white foam on the sand. Although I'd spent very little time at the beach, it was still a soothing sound. It was so familiar it could almost *be* home. Closing my eyes, I breathed deeply. The air here didn't have the salty sting it did on Earth beaches, and I wondered if the water was fresh.

"Vitri, is the ocean here salt water?"

"The water here is full of minerals from the rivers and mountains washed from the island. You can drink it, but the taste is quite strong."

"Is there anything in the water that will kill me?"

"Not while the sun is out. The water is too warm for them this close to shore."

I was already removing my shoes, and, not wanting to get back into wet clothes, I pulled my tunic over my head. Vitri made a sound somewhere between a gasp and growl as I ran toward the water, squealing as the cold waves lapped at my thighs and then my waist. Taking a deep breath, I dove under. The cool water invigorated my pores, stinging only slightly on the cuts and grazes on my legs and arms but soothing the wounds as well, rushing across my skin and reenergizing me. I almost laughed underwater. Not the most graceful swimmer, I burst from the surface, and finding my footing, I then scooped up a handful of the water and lifted it to my lips.

Pulling a face, I smacked my lips together—it tasted like... a cave. There was no other way to describe it. I imagined if I were to find a rock at home and lick it, it would taste like this water. Not sickening, but I wouldn't go out of my way to drink it either. I brushed my fingers slowly through the water, letting it relax me, soothe all my worries and concerns, and try to make this planet feel a little bit more like the home it was apparently destined to be.

It happened too quickly for me to call for Vitri, and I released a strangled cry as I was grabbed.

While I was certain Vitri was watching me being pulled underwater, it filled me with dread faster than the elation that had flooded me a moment earlier. Underwater, I opened my mouth to scream on an instinct I wished I could've controlled, and the rich minerals in the water flooded my mouth. The strong, pungent taste was forced down my throat, and I gagged, closing my mouth even though my lungs screamed at me to take a breath to replace the air I'd lost screaming.

As quickly as I had been pulled under, my head broke the surface again, and I was dragged onto the shore, my hands clawing uselessly at the water to try and get a grip on anything, my toes dragging through the sand underwater. I took only a brief moment to wipe my eyes so I could see before lashing out at my captor. Ahead of me, Vitri was waist-deep in the water where I had been, screaming my name and splashing around. I tried to call out to him but instead began coughing again. The sand gave way under my feet every time I tried to get up, but still, I struggled.

When I was dropped onto the sand, I jumped to my feet after coughing up a mouthful of water and forgot my nudity as I was faced with an unfamiliar creature. His gaze traced my body, although his expression not one of hunger but anger and almost accusation, as though he blamed me for not being whatever he *thought* he was catching. I took a step back, and the creature let me, and I allowed my gaze to trace his body the way he had mine.

Grays, purples, and shimmering skin. Slight frills in his neck that could've been hiding gills with webbed fingers and toes. Four on each hand and foot. Purple shoulder-length hair.

And his eyes.

Bright green eyes.

My mind raced, and I forced myself to calm, remembering the difference between Vitri and his mountain of a brother, Ilk. We were here to meet his brother. So, could this be...

"Sahcor?" I asked, trying my best not to botch the pronunciation. His eyes widened, but he said nothing, and his gaze wandered up and down my naked body again. Throwing my hands up, I took another step backward, turning to find Vitri fighting his way through the water toward me, calling my name and eyeing our visitor wearily. First, Vitri smashes my face into a tree, then Ilk slams me to the ground in the forest, and then I almost drown when this asshole drags me underwater.

"Dammit!" I cried, kicking sand in his direction. "Why can't any of you brothers greet normally? Why must I always be attacked? This is *bullshit.*"

I took a moment to throw a tantrum, no longer feeling threatened by this creature before me, who, with every second that passed, I was increasingly sure was Sahcor. Kicking up sand and throwing my arms up, I repeated my favorite word as Vitri awkwardly splashed his way to shore.

Water was not his element.

After I had expended some excess energy and pulled my tunic back on, I planted my hands on my hips and eyed Sahcor. Still, he said nothing, and although his head didn't move, his eyes would shift to the side, watching Vitri's ungraceful approach before shifting back to me. What I was seeing hit me like a smack in the face, and I took a step backward.

Sahcor was alone.

Fear gripped my stomach.

Where the hell was the girl from the pod?

CHAPTER
26

VITRI

The ocean made moving difficult, and I hated every second of it. I'd dived into the water after Tori had been pulled under, but before I'd even got my footing, unable to keep straight with the waves knocking me about, she was being dragged ashore. Now she was pacing up and down in front of Sahcor, shouting at him and kicking up sand. I hoped he had read the human's mind as I had and was able to understand Tori, and I hoped she was being as fearsome with him as she was when she was mad at me. Sahcor was my brother, but he had attacked my mate, and my heart pounded in my chest as I struggled to keep my breathing under control. The desire to claim Tori again was strong, to show me that she was mine and was safe. I'd fuck her on the sand in front of him to show him she belonged to me and warn him never to touch her again.

Every second it took me to work my way through the water to get to Tori was agony.

"Tori!" When I finally broke free of the trap of the water and slugged my way through the wet sand, I called to her. Tori turned, her short hair whipping around her face and sand streaking her legs and arms. She was breathtaking in her anger, primal, *my mate*.

She met me halfway up the beach, storming over to me. "*Why* do your brothers keep attacking me? First Ilk tackles me to the ground, then this fool..." she pointed her thumb behind her, "... tugs me underwater. Why can't you guys just be... *normal?*"

Without a word, I wrapped my arms around her and yanked her against me. I expected her to struggle, to keep yelling at Sahcor, but instead, she melded against me, sighed loudly, and wove her arms around me in turn. I growled my approval at her affection, unable to keep the smirk from my face.

Over the top of Tori's head, I watched Sahcor, his fingers twitched against his sides and his jaw clenched. He still hadn't said a word, but he was looking at me like Ilk had when we had first reunited. Sahcor was always more patient than us, his control over himself rallying all our brothers, but he was quieter than Ilk in his control. He was an observer who would study the world around him before saying anything.

"What's wrong, Sahcor?" I asked.

He shook his head, a ridged motion, and clenched his jaw further. "You shouldn't be here. There is too much danger already. There are other females."

Tori pulled from my grasp then. "Others who came with me? Yes, I know. Who was with you? Did you see a female like me? Samara? Misha? Are they safe?"

Sahcor eyed her, repeating the words with a growl. "There are *others.*"

"What do you mean?" Tori was yelling again, and Sahcor continued to stand there and take her abuse, his shoulders sagging slightly as though he felt he deserved it.

"He means..." Tori whipped around, her short hair splashing droplets over her face as another female approached. Her hair was dark and curly and fell above her shoulders, but where the sun hit it, it glinted with hints of a deep red. "Other than the four of us, there are other girls. The Ghaal have them. I've seen them."

Tori broke away from me and moved toward her, wrapping her arms around the other female and crushing her against her chest. "Misha, thank fuck you're okay."

Misha's face remained expressionless, and I glanced between her and Sahcor. Something was wrong. I couldn't escape the sense that danger was near, and snarling, I reached out and grabbed Tori's wrist, tugging her away from Misha and back against my body.

My angry growls drowned out Tori's protest. "Something is wrong," I said simply, taking a step back.

"I'm safe, Tori, but you shouldn't have come for me."

"How could I not?" Tori cried before looking at me. "Vitri?" Tori glanced between Sahcor and me, then to Misha, her brows drawing together until she realized we all shared the same grim expression. "Can someone please tell me what the fuck is going on?"

Abruptly, Misha jerked, her spine straightening before her shoulders were pushed back in a violent motion. She dropped to her knees with a cry of pain. Sahcor rushed to her side as Tori called her name, but I didn't let Tori go.

"What's wrong?" Sahcor asked Misha, brushing her hair from her face.

Misha sobbed as she looked down at her arm, a small lump visible under her skin I hadn't noticed before was now flashing intermittently with an orange blinking light. "I think they know she's here," she said, her gaze flickering to Tori. Forcing herself to her feet, Misha offered Tori a sad glance. "The Ghaal tagged me, Tori. I can't stay near you. They'll use me to find you. I'm sorry, you need to go." She took several purposeful steps away from us, shaking her head. "I'm okay, but please leave. Don't follow me."

With that, she turned on her heel and sprinted down the beach.

"Misha!" Tori screamed her name, yanking against my hold on her. *"Let me go."*

Sahcor's look was stony, and when he looked at me, I almost recoiled at the rage in his eyes. "Are you going back to be with our brothers?"

"We were all going to meet and—"

"Go. I'll get Misha, and we'll catch up to you. We'll find a way to remove the tracker."

"Sahcor—"

"*Go,*" he roared and took off after Misha.

Tori stood watching Sahcor and Misha's retreating forms, still squirming against my hold on her arms. "What do we do?"

"We do as he says."

"We can't just leave her."

I worked my jaw as it clenched. "Sahcor will get her."

"Misha said there were other girls..." Tori sounded breathless, no doubt trying to put her thoughts together as I was. This hadn't been the reunion she had hoped for—all hugs and laughter and a small feast.

I swallowed, trying to gather my thoughts when all I could think of was getting Tori far away from here and keeping her safe. "We'll go to Ilk. We'll gather the brothers."

Ilk and I had shared brief thoughts about the need for the Ghaal's reign to end. Maybe now was the time, after all. Moving around for weeks on end, hoping to shake them from our tail wasn't the right move, not this time. Misha had been captured and tagged, and if it weren't for a lone Ghaal with a conscience, Erica would still be a prisoner.

This needed to end.

We'd need weapons and a plan.

Guilt burned in the pit of my stomach that it took Tori and the appearance of the human females to motivate us to take action. We didn't want violence, but being passive to the violence the Ghaal was committing was just as bad. We did our best to keep species away from the colony, but as I told Tori, we couldn't save them all.

Maybe it's time we saved everyone once and for all.

If one species had to be wiped out to save many, then wasn't that for the greater good? I felt I needed Ilk's input. He was more levelheaded, more of a leader, and hopefully less driven by these emotions we've recently rekindled. Sahcor's thoughts would help too, but that could wait until we were reunited at Ilk's. Right now, he needed to calm and look after Misha.

Although with the way Ilk looked at Erica, maybe he wasn't so levelheaded anymore. Maybe he was in as deep as I was.

We'd been moving for days as Ilk and Erica would have been. Had they already found the fourth female who landed with Tori, Erica, and Misha? Maybe it *was* time for us to come together. Waiting longer served no further purpose. Although the selfish part of me wanted to snatch up Tori, run all the way back to the forest, and keep her with me.

I crushed Tori against me, needing to feel her body close to mine.

Because only she could drown out the unfamiliar thoughts of violence that circled my mind.

"When all this is over, what do we do?"

Tori was looking at me earnestly as she spoke. It always caught me off guard when she was like this—the feisty, always-fighting Tori I met becoming unsure of herself.

"What do you want to do?"

Her lip lifted almost into a smirk before sinking back into her worried expression. We'd begun our journey back to Ilk's and were moving slower than we otherwise would, giving Sahcor and Misha time to catch up with us.

"Whatever we want, right?" Tori said.

"Do you think you'll want to live with your friends or me?"

Tori paused, thoughtful for a moment, and I tried not to let concern flood me. Just because she was taking a moment to answer didn't mean she was going to leave me the first chance she got to live with her species. "I'm not sure…" she said finally, looking up at me, "… but we'll figure that bit out. Maybe we can all live together? I don't know. As long as I'm with you, I'll be happy." I was about to respond when she pulled a face, scrunching up her features and sticking out her tongue. "Ugh, that felt weird to say. Much too romantic for me."

I leaned toward her, whispering, "Would it help if I told you I wanted only to fuck you for the rest of my days?"

Tori squirmed as a shiver ran down her spine. "It helps."

"Good," I growled, squeezing her hand. The moment we knew Misha was safe, the *second* she and Sahcor were back with us, I would take Tori off to the side. We'd find a spot to be alone all night, and even that wouldn't be enough.

I'd never get enough of her. But she was mine now, and it was more than I'd thought possible from the day I split from my brothers.

To find a mate made for me.

EPILOGUE

TORI

The complete journey to Ilk's cave would take two days as we had to backtrack the way we had come. Following the beach further toward the base of the mountains and then heading upward would be a mistake as that would put us right in line with the Ghaal colony. The conversation had turned to Vitri's brothers' behavior. I couldn't let go of the fact that my introductions to both of his brothers so far—Ilk and Sahcor—had involved them attacking me.

Honestly, *what the fuck*, right?

Vitri chuckled when I complained about this,

pulled me close to him, and explained why I should cut his brothers some slack. "My mate, remember how I explained to you that your presence here stirred up a part of me I had long forgotten?"

"Yes, but—"

Vitri smiled, placing a large, velvety finger against my lips before using his thumb in an attempt to smooth the frown from my face. "Let me explain."

Fine. I guess I could do that, but I still muttered under my breath, "This is bullshit."

He ignored it, and my lip twitched into a smirk.

"Sahcor and Ilk would be experiencing the same thing, the emotional turmoil, the lust, the conflict of wanting to protect but also feeling a possessiveness they probably feel they should be able to control. It would be particularly hard for Sahcor. If Misha was tagged, that means the Ghaal had captured her at some point like they had Erica." A deep growl rumbled through his chest, and my expression softened. "I wouldn't be able to speak if I lost you. I'd be so angry, they'd have to stop me from killing every one of them."

The visual of Vitri tearing through a village Godzilla-style while little green men—because I'd never seen a Ghaal—flooded my mind. I remembered how Sahcor had held himself, stomping rather than walking, his shoulders and arms tense, his hands curled into fists. He was holding back so much anger and emotion, and all of it spilled forth when Misha collapsed.

But as much as I wanted to give them extra slack for their feelings toward the women, they needed to understand that I had a bond with them too. A bond of the most fucked-up kind, forged by tragedy and insane circumstances we were all forced to deal with.

I wanted them to be safe.

No. I *needed* them to be safe.

Because if, after all of this, I made it, and they didn't just because my pod happened to land near Vitri, I'm not sure I could bear that guilt. So, I said nothing, ground my teeth to bite back the arguments I wanted to spew forth, and allowed Vitri to take my hand and curl his fingers between mine.

We walked. We rested. We ate.

Sahcor and Misha hadn't shown up yet.

Every time I woke during the night with Vitri's chest rising and falling against my back, I'd squint through the swirling dust from the winds, hoping to see their outline in the moonlight.

"They'll come soon, my mate," Vitri muttered sleepily, drawing me closer against him, curling his large form around mine to protect me and remind me I needed to sleep.

I was worried about Samara too. Had Erica and Ilk found her? Ilk seemed certain another brother was near her and would keep her safe. But she seemed so innocent and naïve. What if a Ghaal had come across her first, and she had trusted him?

So now I was worried about Sahcor, Misha, *and* Samara.

And Erica and Ilk.

It felt like no one would be safe while the Ghaal were a threat.

I'd seen only a glimpse of what a Synth was like when they were losing control, and I had no doubt the damage they were capable of if that snap in control was fueled by rage rather than lust. It was painful not being able to take any action. I knew this feeling, an amplified version of when Vitri and Ilk had gone to rescue Erica from the Ghaal, and I was left to wait. I knew this feeling from watching my mother's mind deteriorate and not being able to do a damn thing about it. Misha seemed like a tough girl in the brief and strained encounters we had. But these were extreme circumstances.

We would reach Ilk's soon, then we'll make a plan.

My eyes drifted closed, unable to stay awake any longer.

We moved through a forest of thin, white trees with

feathery leaves that splayed out at the top. Along the way, Vitri stripped some bark from the tree and handed it to me to eat. It was rubbery and difficult, but I was hungry and didn't much care at this point what we ate. I also wanted to rest somewhere where the winds weren't blowing constantly, and Ilk's cave sounded perfect.

I wouldn't say that to Vitri, though. I imagine he would think I was somehow insulting his tree house. But that was far away now, and although the journey would be easy in a car, when we had to walk everywhere, distance looked a lot different.

As we broke out into a field, a creature was barreling toward us. He was the same size as Ilk and similar build, with flat features that also looked to be made of stone. But he was different—angry reds and harsh grays, giving the illusion he was made of cracked stone and streaks of fire.

He looked like a goddamn demon.

Vitri watched the approach with only a curious cock of his eyebrow. My initial urge was to hide behind Vitri, which while I'm sure he wouldn't have minded, it seemed pointless when Vitri didn't appear bothered by this demon giant racing toward us.

I could only assume this was the fourth brother.

Stepping in front of Vitri, I held out my hand, palm toward him, and cried out, "Stop *right* there!"

Vitri looked at me in surprise and even more

shocked when the Synth skidded to a stop. His brow was furrowed, and his green eyes were blazing, matching the deep, heaving breaths and movement of his large chest.

I placed my hands on my hips. "I've had just about enough of being attacked by every single one of Vitri's damn brothers. If you're who I think you are, you can introduce yourself in a civilized manner."

His eyes widened, not in shock but in anger, and his lip lifted into an animalistic snarl. I lowered my hands as he reached over his shoulder, and I frowned. Now he was closer and wasn't moving so fast, I could see two pale arms wrapped around his neck. With a smooth motion, the demon-looking alien lifted a young blonde woman over his shoulder, placed her on her feet in front of me, and shoved her gently.

Samara smiled, whipping her hair over her shoulder and racing the final distance to me. She clamped my arms to my side in a death grip of a hug, and I laughed at her enthusiasm, patting her awkwardly on her lower back with the only motion I could manage the way she was holding me.

When she pulled away, her smile was wide. "Wow, Tori, I love your hair."

I smirked. "You look amazing." And she did with a healthy flush to her cheeks even though they were streaked with dirt. As I pulled Samara in for another hug, a growl came from the alien man behind her, and I raised my eyebrows at him.

"Easy, Lanir, she means no harm," Vitri said, then said something in his native tongue which I assumed was the same message. Lanir's eyes flickered to me but only briefly before settling on Samara again, and his expression softened.

It seemed she had tamed the demon.

"Where's Misha?" Samara asked, looking around.

"On her way."

Samara nodded as Lanir dragged his gaze to Vitri, as if not looking at Samara for one moment was torture for the demon-looking alien. "We're making a plan. Come," he rumbled. Lanir held out his hand for Samara, who looked at me, her eyes wide and unreadable, before she took his hand and followed him back to Ilk's.

"Well…" I said, as Vitri and I followed behind, "…they're a right barrel of laughs."

"They're worried about Misha." Vitri's tone was somber.

I stopped, grabbing his arm. "I *know* that. Don't you think I know that? Don't mistake my sarcasm for apathy. I'm just as worried about my friends as your hulking grumpy-as-fuck brother is."

Vitri sank to a knee and ran his hands up and down my arms. "We'll all be together soon, my mate."

My lip twisted. I almost wanted to correct him. I

didn't feel like his mate anymore, or even his partner, not with the others around. Sahcor had barely acknowledged me. Lanir looked at Vitri rather than both of us, and it felt like Vitri and I couldn't be ourselves with the company like we'd slipped from mates back to friends. Our conversations and interactions were awkward and stilted.

I wanted all the girls to be safe.

But then I think all I really wanted was to be with Vitri.

He watched the emotions swirl around in my expression while continuing to stroke my arms. "We're just about at Ilk's now, and together, we'll figure this all out."

He seemed so sure, and before I felt myself dropping into a pit of self-despair, I took a shuddering and steadying breath. Vitri hadn't let me down to date, and with all of us together, we *would* find and rescue the other girls Misha spoke of.

And if, along the way, we could make sure the Ghaal couldn't hurt anyone else, that would be a bonus. I'm not sure how the Synths felt about that, but part of me simply wanted to eradicate them from the surface of the fucking planet for all they had done. Once everyone was safe, I didn't care what happened to the Ghaal.

What if they also had *other* species captive?

Could we save them too?

I looked at Vitri for answers to questions I couldn't find the will to voice. Not yet, anyway. We would talk about this all together. My alien continued to stare at me earnestly, and I nodded and straightened my shoulders.

This wasn't the time for doubt.

This was the time for action.

And with my mate, Vitri, I was safe, happy, and ready for the next step.

THE END

Continue with...
Redeemer – Elements of Abduction Book 3
for
Samara and Lanir's story

When the grumpy/sunshine dynamic
meets a language barrier,
you'll find Lanir impossible not to love.

ACKNOWLEDGMENTS

This series was exciting for me because the idea of it came to me like a bolt of lightning. And it keeps building. I'm still filling up my notepads and voice recorder with little notes of things to add for the coming books to complete the six-part series.

In fact, I loved the way one of my beta readers put it—*I really thought, I can't get used to new characters! I love Ilk and Erica. Then BAM! Vitri and Tori storm into my heart.*

And I said, *wait until you meet Samara and Lanir.*

I can only hope you love this world and these characters as much as I, that they are as visceral to you as they are in my mind, and that they tug at your heartstrings the same way.

I have a very small circle of people I keep close to me. I thank them in every book because their support never waivers, and they deserve the thanks and more.

Yet every time I sit to write the acknowledgments, I think how awesome would it be to come up with something cool, unique, and creative? Then I blank.

But you know what? That's okay because I'm going to keep thanking the same people since they're still here for me. They never left. They stayed through all the millions of questions I had, through my doubts, through very one-sided conversations where I talked through a plot point or hole only to interrupt myself with "Never mind, I figured it out!"

They believed in me, even when I didn't.

A special thank you to Kay and Ashleigh first off for your absolute belief in this series, and encouragement to not only keep going with it but to do what I needed to do to streamline the release.

Thank you to Kate, Chris, and Kim. I hope you never tire of my relentless questions and the accompanying self-doubt because they go hand-in-hand.

And always, *always,* thank you to Jason. I'll never name a character after you because nothing I create can do you justice. Besides, this way, I get to keep you all to myself.

But I hope you know how thankful and grateful I am for you and how incredible you are.

ANGELS AND FIRE BOOKS

Find our exciting stories at:

www.angelsandfirebooks.com.au

READER GROUP

Want access to fun, prizes and sneak peeks?

Rescuer

Join my Facebook Reader Group.
https://www.facebook.com/groups/588038442170571

NEWSLETTER

Sign up for my Newsletter.
https://www.subscribepage.com/angelsandfirebooks

BOOKBUB

https://www.bookbub.com/authors/stefanie-dawn

GOODREADS

Add my books to your TBR list
on my Goodreads profile.
https://www.goodreads.com/author/
show/21761217.Stefanie_Dawn

AMAZON

https://www.amazon.com/author/stefaniedawn

WEBSITE

http://www.angelsandfirebooks.com.au/

INSTAGRAM

https://www.instagram.com/angelsandfirebooks

EMAIL

info@angelsandfirebooks.com.au

FACEBOOK

https://www.facebook.com/stefaniedawnwriter

ABOUT THE AUTHOR

Stefanie Dawn has been a writer and creative soul all her life **and** strives to give her readers stories they can escape into as they become absorbed in the worlds created.

When she isn't writing, Stefanie might be painting, reading, or watching movies. She loves the process of producing films as another form of storytelling. There's also a good chance she'll be baking some delicious treats—pretending she won't later regret consuming them—or simply enjoying a cocktail with friends.

Stefanie Dawn lives in South Australia with her ever-supportive partner and a lovable gang of rescue cats.

You can stay up to date with
Stefanie and her books at:
www.angelsandfirebooks.com.au

www.ingramcontent.com/pod-product-compliance
Lightning Source LLC
Chambersburg PA
CBHW051137190726
48290CB00006B/1884